*Also by the author:*

*In a Cosmic Egg* (poetry) Finishing Line Press (2012)
*Disturbed Sleep* (flash fiction) FutureCycle Press (2013)
*Many Worlds: Some American Odysseys* Shanti Arts (2020).

# MADNESS WITH GRIEF

## M. Kaat Toy

**Livingston Press**

**The University of West Alabama**

Library of Congress Control Number 2021945748

Typesetting and page layout: Joe Taylor
Proofreading: Tricia Taylor, Lauren Fuller, Cailtin Saxon, Lauren Fuller,
Hilary Nelson, Brooke Barger
Cover Art and Illustrations: Katherine Toy Miller

Cover self-portrait was published as "A Good Time" in Paper Radio number 12, spring/summer 1995. Print. Part Three image was published as "In the People's Art Museum" in Art Mag issue 18, summer 1995. Print. A reading from Madness with Grief by Katherine Toy Miller with Vance Bourjaily, October 19, 1981, is available at voca, the University of Arizona Poetry Center's Audio Video Library, voca.arizona.edu. "Madness Stories" in The Hunger, online fall 2018. "Lost Celestials" in Midway Journal, online December 2010/January 2011. "The Stone Father" in West Wind Review, 26th edition, December 2007. "Swish," "The Fish," "Tyro," and "Sailing" as "Mild Vertical Drifting" in Midway Journal, online October 2007. "Evolution" in Sojourner, July 1990. "Rude" in Shankpainter, spring 1989. "Substituting" in The Nebraska Review, fall 1987. "Shopping" in Lactuca, November 1987. "Saved Again" in The Small-Towner, April 1986. "Banking" in Tongue, fall 1986. "Life Drawing," "Swept Away," and "Parties for Eleanor" in Green Feather Magazine, 1986. "Tribal Medicine" in Other Voices, winter 85-86. "Biting the Glass" in The Apalachee Quarterly, numbers 23-23, 1985. "A Good Time" in Permafrost, spring 1984. The quote on "autism" is from Merriam Webster's Medical Dictionary, 1995, online.

# MADNESS
# WITH
# GRIEF

"Family life is easy./You just push off into heartbreak and go on your nerve."

—William Matthews in *A Happy Childhood*

# AUTHOR'S NOTE

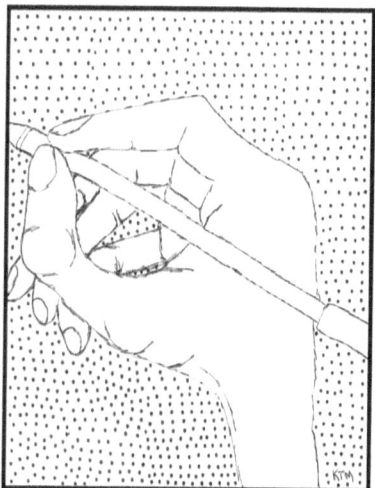

When I was five years old I thought all the books in the world were written by God. I didn't think a human being was capable of doing anything that miraculous. Now I know people write books and not God, though my main character, Eleanor, seems to me to be a gift from God and to have nothing to do with me though almost everything I say she has done, I have done.

In my graduate workshop the professor asked, "What is the plot of this novel?" The whole class wanted to know.

"Eleanor gets better," I said, which seemed to me a surprisingly brilliant answer.

"That's not a plot," they said condescendingly.

*It isn't?* I thought, looking at them. *Why isn't it?* What was better, hero spends ten years journeying home fighting Gorgons and Harpies? It had drama, suspense, action. It led to a conclusion unknown even to me.

*Eleanor gets better.* It sounded like a plot to me, and if it wasn't, I knew I was lost, but I didn't think I was lost. I thought everyone else was.

When a fellow student, Karl, stopped me in the hallway and asked, "How's Eleanor?" I said, "She's fine." I knew he didn't mean how was I doing or how was my novel going. He was asking about the health of my character. Karl was the resident geek. He fancied himself a literary lady's man on his good days; other days he was just a scrawny drunk guy with bad teeth and writer's block.

"I mean, how is she *really*?" he said, or something like that.

"She's fine."

"Well, tell me about her. Is she cute? What does she look like?"

The way he was asking made me feel protective of her.

"I don't know. I guess she looks like me," I said though I knew she didn't.

"Well, do you think she would go out with me?" he asked.

Then I really felt protective. I knew he didn't want to go out with me. He was afraid to take me on. He thought Eleanor would be easier.

"She's someone I made up, Karl."

"Yeah, but I'd like to go out with her. Do you think I could?"

"No, Karl."

"But I'd really like to."

"You *can't* go out with her," I finally said. "She's not *real.*"

But I felt like I had betrayed her when I said she was not real, and I thought that was a good sign.

# PART ONE

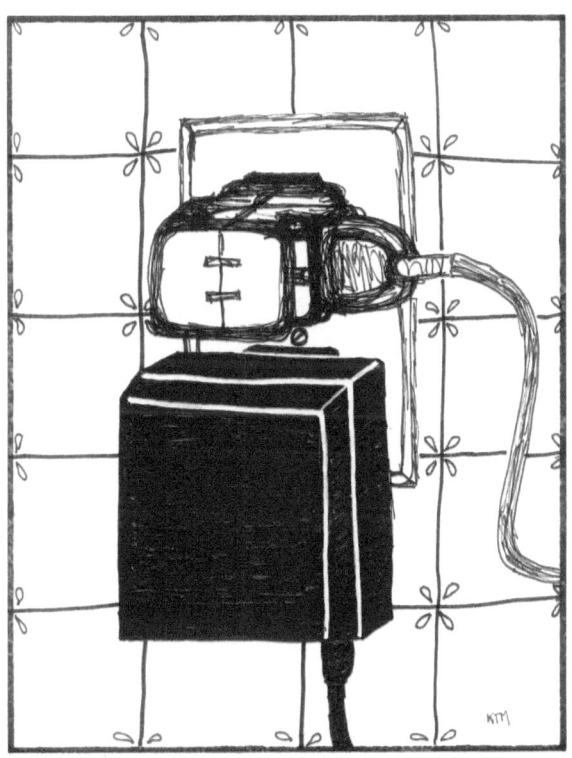

One winter night during Eleanor's senior year in college she and her brother Teddy, older by two years, stood in the institutional light of their central California home propped up by the green-tiled kitchen counter. Actually they were sloping, on very separate places, against the counter which curved around the intensely familiar kitchen.

Eleanor felt the air of intimacy was strong enough to bend light. The scene, to her, appeared as if reflected in an insect-eyed surgical light. Knowing their parents were out, they had coincidentally returned—she from her academic absences, Teddy from the prolonged nearness of his house in town. This meeting in the presence of queer angles of light was a rare chance for her to question her brother aided by an atmosphere of drunkenness and calculation.

She went into the den, removed a plaque from the wall, and returned holding it closely, knowing Teddy knew what the plaque said: "Third Place. California High School Music Awards. James Jasper Lihte. Saxophone."

Mornings when she was ten, she would finish her breakfast as her big brother, Jamie, older by eight years, rangy and remote, walked in rubbing his dark eyes, tired from late nights practicing with his rock band, Lost Celestials. He was their leader. After school he was the drum major on the football field. But in the mornings he was simply late.

"You're burning the candle at both ends!" their mother would scream at him, as if it were unnatural, as if it were something criminals did to escape.

Eleanor laid the plaque on the counter. "I've been thinking how different we might be if Jamie wouldn't have died."

The events in their lives were probably explainable, justifiable, not really negative at all when viewed with the proper attitude, having a bright side, a silver lining, she thought. Perhaps the silver lining was the lure of death, she considered, conceded.

Teddy shrugged his shoulders, threw back his head, and took a long swallow from his beer. He put down the empty can.

She continued. "If he would have finished college then you might have finished. It would have been different if he would have been around, if he would have made it through, don't you think?"

Teddy shrugged again and opened the refrigerator. She moved to help him, slipping a beer can from her hand into his then moving back.

"We might have all been teachers," she said. "If Jamie were teaching music, and I were teaching, you might have gone into teaching."

Teddy smiled a little then popped the top.

"I guess it doesn't matter. At least you're making money. Do you like working for Dad?" Their formidable father was a contractor, the best around people said.

"It's all right. It's pretty hard, but it's not as bad as people think."

She picked up his ashtray. Dampening her finger under the water tap then dipping it into the ashes, she drew a thick black trail that curved at each bend of the counter, replenishing the mixture each time the streak began to thin.

He extinguished his cigarette under the faucet and got another ashtray from the windowsill.

"I was thinking of going to Jamie's grave," she said. "Have

you ever been back?"

"Shit," he responded, then walked to the dining room table to look at the mail.

She dipped her finger into the water and ashes again. "Just thought I'd ask. No one ever talks about him. Mom and Dad won't talk about him. I feel bad asking them. I think they feel guilty."

"They don't feel guilty. It wasn't their fault. They loved him more than anyone."

*We all loved him more than anyone*, she thought.

"You don't really blame them, blame them for what happened, do you?" he asked.

*Of course. Of course not. It was the fault of the number line that reached out from the kitchen corner of this house into infinity.*

Sentences dissipated in the air between Eleanor and her brother.

"Why do you think Mother and Dad had those football players live here after Jamie died? Don't you think it was strange?" she asked.

From when she was eleven until she was fifteen, her father invited home a good-looking football player from the junior college to placate their mother, to take Jamie's place.

"They thought it would be good for us. They did it to help us. They didn't think about it. And there was room."

*Of course. There was room. The house was obligated to fill itself, to make room for the needy.*

Teddy came into the kitchen, picked up his beer, and turned toward the sink, sucking slowly. She realized she would never know in what ways he was lying. She asked why her displays of affection, her questions about his work and social life, her interest in what magazines he preferred caused him to become angry, preparing for his answer by concentrating on the loud buzz of the light overhead, forcing herself to become intrigued with its glare.

"It's not you. It's just that first it was Jamie then Grandpa. You know how they used to say, 'He's his grandpa's boy,' the big deal about Grandpa."

She nodded. Teddy, born on their mother's father's birthday, the only child their mother saw something of herself in. Their grandfather had paid special attention to him, but their grandfather died the year after Jamie did.

"Then it was Greg. When I heard about him, smashed inside his car, his dog standing guard outside, that was it. I just didn't care anymore." He bent his head back, sucking his beer. Greg was his college best friend.

She had forgotten so much, not counted so many things. That was why it never added up. She remembered Teddy coming home from work one summer afternoon, changing his clothes, going to Greg's funeral, then going back to work. That fall he moved out and didn't go back to college. He had been studying drawing.

She thought she would make Teddy cry by asking him questions. She thought that was why he wouldn't talk. But now as tears ran out from underneath her hands, he didn't cry at all. In her mind she argued with him though, insisting he have a different response, one more like her own, that he fan Jamie's black mark and suck on the dying smoke.

She felt herself slipping to the floor, down the smooth white wooden cupboard door as she did as a child. Sitting there, slumped and undisturbed, she looked at the linoleum and remembered the death of her brother as marked by lemonjellocake, marshmallowfruitsalad, boredom and emotional roulette, her grandmother's bright red coat at the funeral. A time of confidences thrust upon her.

She watched Teddy put his beer can in the trash. As he put on his coat, she stood and followed him out to the patio.

"Remember that time Mother brought home that cake on your birthday?" she asked.

"And I asked if she bought it because she was having *company,*" he replied.

"And she got mad and said no, it was for you," she answered.

They laughed. For their mother, company came first, then their father, then the kids.

Teddy picked up an orange from a sack on the barbecue table and tossed it to her, a singularly friendly gesture. As he crossed the yard, she tossed it back. He walked out to the driveway, and she stood at the gate, her hands on the metal crossbar, watching as exhaust rose off the tailpipe of his red Porsche, and he disappeared into the dark.

She imagined a parade of little cars trailing him down the hill, then circling back, not really wanting to leave, having merely felt obligated because of the parents and the hour. Parked in a line, their doors swung open like chorus girls' legs, and leather-clad young men hopped out. It was a magic show as the girls swung their legs back into position, and the men mounted motorcycles and turned in tight circles. Smiling and turning on bright yellow motorcycles, they dipped and curved in giant slalom passes; then, in pairs, they swooped through each other in double-crossing figure eights. There were magenta streamers on the handlebars and packs of cards distributed on the spokes, and the effervescent men wore black leather and blended into the night, leaving only smiles and white headlights and yellow motorcycles and magenta streamers.

In a lighted stadium the young men lined up wearing white football uniforms with gold numbers, holding their matching helmets at their sides as they stood ready for the band leader to pass. Dressed in gold and white, he wore a drum major's busby hat nearly as high as his baton and carried a saxophone to one side. The men fell in behind him, marching and twisting and high-stepping for her pleasure, until the band leader moved them too quickly off the field, and she was left with her white and purple hand upon the gate.

That summer Eleanor found herself living in her parents' big white house on the hill. She had expected to be married and settled by now, but, as her father pointed out at her graduation, she didn't have a boyfriend or a career. Instead, she lifeguarded at the public pool outside of town. She had always worked, but she thought of work as something to do until her real life came along. Now her real life was here, and she was surprised by how disappointing it was. She gave herself until the age of twenty-five; then, if her life hadn't improved, she would either invest her savings in surgical breast implants to make her bust line more pleasing or put a pistol to her head and blow her brains out, which was what she dreamed of.

In the morning when she arrived on her bike, seeing the pool sparkle gently like a pale blue jewel cheered her, but by afternoon its surface glared fiercely in the heat trapped under a dome of hazy western sky. The dry but fertile valley her family had lived on for three generations was ringed by mountains that shut out the rain. All day she skimmed away piles of crickets and June bugs that came in from the fields. Tar-splattered oil field trucks passed by and farm trucks overflowing with cotton, cantaloupe, or chickens in their cages. Heavy-bellied crop dusters raced over miles of uniformly green rows, dropping powdery white pesticides or oily herbicides. The hot winds smelled of sulfur, cow manure, and rotted onions.

"What happened to my happy little girl?" her mother asked when Eleanor came home tired and discouraged.

"It's too bad you're a girl," her father said. "Otherwise we could make a place in the business for you. You could be making money like your brother Teddy."

As a child she had wanted to be a lifeguard like her brother Jamie. She loved watching him, handsome and cocky with his white teeth and dark tan, flirting with the girl guards in their white suits and blowing his whistle at the kids. At dinner he peeled his burnt shoulders, laughing at their mother's disgust.

Now she stood roasting on the same deck, a whistle in her hand, but pretending, uncertain. In all her years of lifeguarding, she had never saved anyone. The opportunity had not presented itself though she tried to stay ready in case it did. She thought it might give her life meaning and worth. Besides, she had been trained for it: "Tow, throw, row, and go!"

Ever since Jamie died she had been trying to rescue him, to pull him back at the moment before his crash, but she had no training for that. It took a month for him to die of the injuries to his head. For those four weeks, she studied the pictures and articles in the town paper telling of his life and deteriorating condition, then of his funeral arrangements. Her parents refused to talk about him.

In the coffin, his face was reconstructed where it had smashed through the windshield. No longer ruddy and strong, it was pink, the color of a woman's pancake make-up.

"It's not him! He doesn't look like that!" she had screamed.

Her parents stepped away from her as she looked up at them; then, she stepped closer to her big brother than she had dared to for a long time. For months after, when she set the table, she'd set it for five instead of four. Her mother would have to correct her. Like a buoy, she marked the place where he went down, not letting her family forget.

At the pool her job in the morning was to clean the bathrooms. The kids left socks and gum wads for her to find there. "Faggot Face" and other things were written on the mirrors in soap. She destroyed them with her squirt bottle of ammonia. Whenever the kids saw her washing the mirrors or the windows, they asked what she was doing. She always explained. She thought perhaps they really didn't know. Their lives in their wooden shack houses seemed so different from hers.

While she hosed down the deck, the kids came to stare at the pool and the water being sprayed around. They liked watching the water better than watching TV. But when the kids chased each other down the sloped roof of the visitors' area or spit tobacco on its walls, she had to tell her boss, Mary Jo. Mary Jo's job was to send the kids home.

When the children came to Eleanor with their arguments and problems, she didn't know what to do or what to tell them to do, just as her mother hadn't known what to do when Eleanor and her brothers turned to her.

"I can't take care of everything!" her mother had shouted.

When Jamie died, Eleanor's job was to take care of her mother. Having no one else to go to, they turned to each other, patting each other's backs, glad for the chance to cry. But a lifeguard wasn't supposed to cry—a lifeguard was supposed to know what to do—though Eleanor couldn't understand why suddenly she was expected to. All her life, her mother had told her she was absolutely wrong about everything.

Whenever she could, she retreated to the locker room office where she ate grapes and read what the children's librarian recommended. She was thinking of becoming a grade school teacher. Mary Jo didn't like to read though she liked watching Eleanor read. It made her feel superior. She thought her life was more real than Eleanor's. When they discussed it, Eleanor agreed. Mary Jo's life revolved around softball.

One day when Eleanor was working inside the office, a little boy with a shaved head approached the counter.

Standing on his toes he asked, "Can I trade this mask for a Coke?"

"We own the masks and the boards so you can trade for those, but you have to have fifty cents to get a Coke," she explained.

"But I do have fifty cents," he answered.

He didn't look like he had another fifty cents, but, admiring his persistence, she said, "Okay. Where is it?"

"It's down there." He pointed underneath the counter to the jar of rental money. "I gave you my fifty cents to pay for the mask, and now it's down there. Would you get it for me so I can get a Coke?"

"You can't have that money. That money's already spent. It's gone."

"But it's not gone. It's right down there."

"Yes, but you spent that money once, and now it's not yours. You can't spend it again." She thought of her own money. She was not supposed to spend it. She was supposed to save it and ask her parents for what she needed or do without.

"But I had to spend the fifty cents to get the masks, and now I need the fifty cents to get a Coke." He stood looking at her, skinny in torn shorts, with hours left of the afternoon heat.

"That's the way it is. You have to decide," she told him, thinking of her life and how she had spent it. She had spent it trying to understand the rules; then, she thought of her parents. They were business people. They would be proud of the answers she had given.

When she lifeguarded, Eleanor wore a white one-piece suit that curved up at the legs and dipped down in the front. In the office she put shorts over it. When everyone left she wore her bikini. One day it lay on the counter, an incomprehensible series of triangles and strings, when a man with a huge leather sack belly stretched full of beer, huge brown working man's arms, and a huge brown forehead unlined by thought came in with two small children. Eleanor was intrigued. Her father had been too busy working to spend time with his kids.

"What's that?" the man said, pointing to her bikini.

"It's my bathing suit," she answered with an unfortunate giggle.

"Why don't you put it on for me?" he responded with an encouraging nod.

"I don't want to. I'm not supposed to wear it. I already have my bathing suit on."

"Go on. Put it on," he kept saying.

"I'm not going to. I don't want to," she told him. She looked from his face to his children, uncomfortable they knew this much about him.

At last he left, pushing his boy and girl toward the men's dressing room, saying to them so she could hear, "That girl won't put her little bitty bathing suit on for Daddy. What do you think of that? She won't put it on. And I bet she'd look real pretty in it."

Eleanor was confused. Perhaps this kind of father was harmless after all.


Often Eleanor talked to a girl just graduated from high school who lay out in her cut-off jeans, a shirt tied around her bulging bra top, her soft reddish-brown hair curled, watching her younger brother and sister. Her girlfriends stopped by on their motorcycles or horses and talked to her through the chain-link fence. She talked only of where her boyfriend was taking her for the weekend, how she was going to get her mother to let her out of the house, what house she was going to get her boyfriend to buy. She seemed so sure. She knew what to do.

Four years before when Eleanor graduated high school, she had moved with a friend to the big city nearby, but the friend found a lover and was hardly ever home. Eleanor lifeguarded on the bad side of town. Driving home late in her bathing suit, policemen would stop her, making her open her trunk to see if something stolen was in there. There never was.

One night a boy asked if she would go out with him. She said no. But the next night he asked again, and she said yes. It wasn't really a date because she worked late and they had nowhere to go, but she let him drive her car to a park to make out. When he started pulling off her shorts, she didn't want to make out any more, so she told him to stop and shoved him to the other side of the car.

"I want to go home," she said, but since he was driving she had to convince him to take her.

"You're crazy," he said.

"Just take me home." She straightened her clothes and sat by the door.

"All right, I'll take you home." He revved the engine and raced out of the park, burning rubber. He screeched through a bad neighborhood and threatened to kick her out. She hoped he wouldn't steal her car. Her father would be mad.

Finally he pulled into his driveway, got out, and slammed the door.

She drove home. She sat in her apartment then heard pounding on the door.

"Let me in," he said.

"No."

He kept pounding and trying to break in. She took the phone into her bedroom, shut the door, and shoved her dresser against it. She heard him pounding at the window. She called the police.

"Please, someone is trying to break in," she said.

"Are they in the house?" the dispatch woman asked.

"No, not yet."

"Then there's nothing we can do."

"Please, he's trying to break in."

"Okay. We'll send someone out."

Eleanor hid in the closet until the pounding went away, then went into the living room. She watched the clock. After two hours the police came.

"I know his name. I know his address. He was trying to break in."

"Did he get in?"

"No."

"Then there's nothing we can do."

"But he's trying to get me."

"Sorry."

"I went out with him tonight; then, he came over and tried to break in."

"Why don't you go out with some nicer guys?" They laughed.

She started crying. They turned and left. She kept crying. She wanted to call her parents, but they would say what had happened was her fault. She fell asleep on top of her bed.

In the morning she called in sick. She wanted to go home. She couldn't afford gas, so she rode her bike. It was forty miles and hot, over one hundred degrees. She'd never ridden that far and didn't have anything to carry water in. Halfway there she lay down beside the road but soon felt better and went on.

When she got home, there was a family barbecue. Her male cousins kissed her. Her mother apologized for not inviting her. Her father patted her on the back and said, "You tired?" and laughed at her.

Teddy said hello as he put his plate on the table. His soft brown hair and big shoulders faced her.

When the party was over, someone offered to drive her home. She didn't tell anyone what had happened. *You're just always unhappy*, her mother would have said.

During this season in the sun Eleanor realized why her job was not glamorous. She and Mary Jo were more like seminude janitors than heroes, guarding against long hair and baby oil in the pool, averting skinned knees by shouting at people running on the deck, and discouraging kids from breaking their faces by yelling at them for jumping from the one-meter board to the gutter's edge.

When a group of kids arrived for a birthday party, Eleanor watched them hanging on the divider rope, going off the boards, splashing in the shallow end if they didn't know how to swim, anxious for her duty to end. A little boy shot down the curving slide and dropped to the bottom of the pool where he sat cross-legged, arms moving slowly.

"Can he swim?" she shouted from the lifeguard tower.

The children were too young to answer. So, disregarding the main rule of her training, which was to go in as a last resort, she stood on the tower rungs and dove. She swam across the pool, took one breath, and headed down. She saw the little boy smiling at her, grabbed his arm, and pulled him toward her. Her feet hit the bottom, and she pushed off with enough strength to shove him onto the deck.

She hung on the gutter, looking up at him. He sat hunched over, sputtering and wiping his eyes.

"Can you swim?" she asked.

"No." He looked at her as if she were stupid.

"Then why did you go off the slide? You knew it was deep water."

"I knew you would come get me."

She didn't answer. She couldn't imagine having that much faith in anyone.

Later she thought about what had happened. She had rescued someone. She had known what to do.

Every day in the office and on the deck, five or six guys just old enough to drive and not yet able to afford it were hanging around, hanging around Eleanor, playing and talking in sexually confident poses. In some ways she liked it.

Once when her hour in the office was nearly up, she got ready to go outside. Pulling at the buckle on her shorts, she noticed a crowd gathering. She turned to them.

"What do you need?" she asked, then observed their faces— Cal, Darrell, Jimmy, the two Johns, Terry. Smiling inwardly, they leaned against each other, trading their weight on their feet, the six of them so big they covered the counter.

"Do you need something?" she asked again.

"Yeah," Cal said with a big mouthful of smile. Slender and confident, he reminded her of Jamie. "Go ahead."

"Go ahead what?"

"Go ahead and take off your pants." He grinned. "That's what you were doing, you were taking them off."

He was right. She was still playing with the buckle.

"You've got to go out, so you've got to do it."

All their faces told her she did. But not yet. There were some minutes left.

"What are you doing?" she said with a one-sided smile. "Why are you all in here?"

"We came to watch you take off your pants," Cal answered. "We do it every day."

"You get out of the pool and wait around just to see me take off my shorts?" She watched their tough young faces as they nodded, vaguely remembering that yes, they did.

So she took them off, turning so they could see the buckle drop open and the buttons unhook, spreading in a "V" down the fly, her white suit shiny tight underneath. She looked up, trying to decide what she felt.

Finally she said to them, "What am I going to do when I leave here? Where am I going to find six guys who care enough to come in and watch me take off my clothes?"

Late one afternoon Cal and another boy walked into the office with their muscular tans, oil-hardened jeans, and empty beer cans. The oil field gang truck had dropped them off. They needed a ride home to get their bathing suits. Eleanor felt scared, but she wanted to make them happy, so she went to ask Mary Jo if she could take them. Mary Jo said okay.

In the parking lot Eleanor saw that the boys had picked up her little yellow car and turned it around, ready to go. She tried to be pleased along with them except the tires were smeared into the ground where they had not been able to lift but only to drag the front end around. She unlocked her door, got in, then looked at them through the glass. No longer smiling, she watched black prints bloom against the windshield as they banged on it with their fists. She paused, then unlocked the doors. They climbed in, yelling and pounding on the seats, then slouched under her disapproval.

A few days later she yelled at a little boy walking through

the staff door of the office, though she had let Cal and some older boys in that way.

"You'd better get out of here," she said to him.

The older boys stood at the counter, pulling their knives on each other and arguing about why they had failed history or math.

She said to the little boy, "You'd better stay away," and he moved back one step.

"You'd better watch out or you'll end up like these guys," she continued, surprised at herself.

But she liked watching him as he backed out the door and said so everyone could hear, "You don't want to end up like them," referring to their stitch-scarred stomachs and eyebrows, their jobs in the oil fields, the tobacco juicing out of their mouths.

"Hell," said Cal, "I didn't want to end up like us."

Suddenly she understood the boys much better.


Some times in Eleanor's life seemed unredeemable, like useless strips of clear plastic curling, turning brown on a table, foreign and inorganic. That fall the storm clouds had begun gathering low and black; the branches of dead trees loomed overhead, suffocating and black; the ground itself seemed overhead and unreachable. When she substituted at her old high school, she felt it was too bad she had grown beyond the confines of her bedroom. When she wanted to see Fireman Rick, she felt it was too bad she was still sleeping in her blue child's room.

One early spring Monday while substituting in biology, she clandestinely reminisced. There was little more to do besides write notes to the principal. Occasionally she looked down to check her cleavage. Things like that let her know she was all right:

She cared what the kids thought, was thinking what they might be thinking, and was concerned with keeping their talking down, their paper airplane throwing, their seat jumping. The kids liked her, they said, not because she was cool, which was what she had hoped, but because they could see down the front of her baggy tops. "Loose Shirts" they called her in their private circles.

Today two students had gone out the third-floor classroom window, diving onto the window ledge and back onto the counter before going on to the principal's office. The class was quiet afterward, and there was time for sketching the clothes she would be sewing, time for the thinking the sketching and sewing allowed.

She thought about dates she had had and dates she would like to have. She thought about the student, sixteen years old, sitting three seats from her. During another class he had come to her desk and announced loudly, "I want to go out with you. I've got a truck. I could take you out."

"No, I can't," she had to tell him and the other students watching. "You're too young. Besides," she said with an inappropriate smile, "I'm your teacher."

She liked him and thought he was nice, nicer than Fireman Rick.

She thought about Fireman Rick and their commitment to indifference. It was an easy commitment to make but not always satisfying. Being left alone was satisfying but being lonely was not. She thought about seeing him on Saturdays, say, for one-half hour, he in official blue offering her copies of *How to Prevent Fires in Your Home* and *The Dangers of Gasoline Transference*, she bouncing on her tiptoes in her short-shorts, scrambling the ends of his curly blond hair, poking at him, and giggling stupidly as his cold-eyed captain—her mother's cousin—watched.

"Don't act so crazy," Fireman Rick would say.

"But if I wasn't crazy, I wouldn't be here," she would answer.

And here in this class of friendly and observant faces, she thought maybe she was tired of spending one-quarter of the night with Rick on occasional Tuesdays after his weekly worship with the men of his ward. She was maybe tired of those hours before 11 p.m. when she cruised Center Street waving at her students and of those hours after 11 p.m. when she found him drinking at The Oasis with his Mormon fireman friends. "Captain Rick and his All-Leather Review," they called themselves. But maybe she was just tired of sewing.

The bell rang. Third period was over. She went to monitor gym. The bell rang again before she could get there. She ran inside to get the roll book and equipment, greeting the teachers who had hated her for being uncoordinated in their classes four years before, then stood outside shouting forty-seven names bringing most of the students back.

"Where'd you get the skinned knee, teacher?" one boy asked.

"Roller-skating."

"Teach-er fell down roll-er-ska-ting," the students mocked.

She tried to look at them sternly, closed the roll book, and laughed.

Half the class was supposed to play softball. The other half was supposed to play volleyball. No one wanted to play volleyball. They bartered with her. She got confused. Brady Jones stuck his face into hers, making lizard motions with his tongue, nearly licking her. He was hyperactive and liked to forget to take his medicine, which for her was a problem. When he remembered it he became soft and huggable with his soft brown hair and soft brown eyes, which for her was also a problem.

She hated softball. She could not keep score. She gave the roll book to one girl to keep track of who left during class. She handed the scorecard to another girl and the card with the batting order to the girl's friend.

In the beginning Eleanor had done all the work—the scorecards, batting order, roll book, absence slips, tardy slips, behavior slips—until someone threw a softball in from the outfield, and she couldn't move fast enough because of all the paperwork and got hit on the shin. The students thought it was funny. Now she could watch the softball and the volleyball though she no longer had control over the roll book or the game scores. No one else would substitute in physical education, so she did. She sewed shorter dresses and ones with narrow straps, so she could get a better tan while teaching now, while thinking about Rick. She thought, *I am sick of this, and you must be sick of this, dear Rick. For me it is always: I'll wait. I'll cry, but I'll be here, and I'll wait. And for you it must always be this: she is crying and waiting.*

During her free period she copied the scores in her own handwriting—two to three, two to zero, six to fourteen—and thought about Rick: *I want to be waiting in the messy kitchen of your two-bedroom, three-bachelor apartment, Rick, waiting for you to come home. I want to wait among the bamboo shades and stolen stop signs, bags of fireman rescue equipment packed to go, and motorcycle parts. It will be eight o'clock, and dinner will have been waiting on the table since six o'clock. I will be the third wife in your life, and you will eat and afterwards, fat, play your flute badly on the green plastic ottoman in front of the TV before going out drinking with your Mormon roommates, and I will watch and wait, through the dinner and the drinking.*

She wondered why she wanted to do that, and why, instead, she spent the weekends moving from her sewing machine to the ironing board to the bed and the cat. The cat was huge and orange, and when she screamed that wide oval kind of scream her mouth got stuck into while she cried, cried because she was lying on the bed alone, and he started getting wet, splashed with tears on the back and in one ear, he sank all of his front toes, each claw as sharp as a bird's beak, into her thigh, and ran, crying at the door until she let him out.

Her mother would open the shut door and say, "Why are you crying, dear? Come help me with dinner. There are some nice rolls you can make. I don't think you know why you're crying anyway, and you're getting spots on the bed. Come make these rolls. Your father will appreciate it. He's going to be home soon, and he'll be hungry. Why don't you put your sewing away for today and help me?"

Eleanor would nod, rub her eyes, and say, "Okay. You're right. I'll help you with dinner. Everything's okay."

She listed her choices: (1) to be freaking, freaking, freaking on her blue floral bed in a room decorated with her name on the door and her mother's leftover lamps, leftover vases, leftover paintings, all very nicely done, stately. Or (2) to hold one thought in her head like a cure. One, such as thinking things would be all right with Rick, or thinking she would see him soon, or thinking she would never see him again. Then (3) she remembered hearing the kids describe each other, and for a moment she thought Rick, too, was a "moist clam." "Moist," they said with disgust, referring to someone's brain.

A baseball bat bounced on the concrete floor behind her. She swiveled in her chair.

"We just wanted to get the ball and play until class starts," a boy said while he and his friend looked through the office window into the girls' dressing room.

"No. Get out of here. You know you're not supposed to be in here," she yelled.

They ran, turning to see her bend over, she watching them and picking up the bat, holding the deep "V" of her blouse to her chest.

Signing roll sheets and absence forms, she pictured herself running cheerfully to the phone three days from now on Thursday, and it was Rick calling, spontaneous Rick. They would date, go to movies, go dancing, have social acceptance, love. But then it was Monday, and he hadn't called, hardly ever called. And she talked to him last on Friday, Friday. She counted the days until Thursday, Thursday and the days since Friday, and tried to calm down, elaborating a sense of security from the fact he would call by Thursday if only she would not panic, run to his door, apartment B, the far end of town, up the sidewalk, trying to act like she belonged there. But the Thursday call was not a fact. The sense of security and the Thursday call were not a reality.

Here's how it was on Sunday afternoons. Her mother would watch as Eleanor leaned over her sewing machine, bumping her head on the levers. "I wish I were as talented as you are, dear," her mother would say.

When her mother stopped staring and left, Eleanor prayed for Rick and herself and peace and love then took two aspirin and a nap with the cat. She prayed: "Oh dear God, let me fit. Let me be relaxed and cool and waiting here all afternoon. Let me not be waiting here but just being here. Make me sweet."

The bell sounded again. Susie and Lori were in this class. Sometimes they asked her out, and though she might want to, because she was their teacher, she couldn't go. They asked her to their softball games.

"Hi, Loose Shirts," they said today. "Tell us where you live. Give us your phone number. We want to visit you."

"No," she had to say.

In the dressing room they called her over.

"I'll give you a dollar," Susie said, "if you tell me where you live. A dollar. Just tell me."

"No."

They gave her a candy bar and a note. "We love you," it said.

She ate the candy bar while watching softball.

"We want some. We want some," everyone said.

On the back of the note she drew a tall thin model in a striped dress. After two more bells and shouting roll, she could go home to sew and think about Rick.


That evening biking through the green fields was tender; riding along the highway expanded in the near-dark. Slipping through the old gentle hills, all her noisy thoughts were pulled away, especially when she peaked at the top of the round soft-colored space between the hills. Only rabbits were brushing between the dust-muted colors. Greens, grays, browns, lavender, blue, orange—the colors were full and rich with dust. They slipped into each other like bands of the rainbow from dirt to stems to sky, becoming the blue night that turned black around the hills. *The people, they can get you in their cars by running you into the rocks and sticker sand,* she thought, *but they cannot get you. The people in the cars don't know you, and they glide past.*

Now it was Saturday, days or weeks later, and she woke early because Rick had invited her, in lieu of something on Friday night, something respectable, something conventional, to visit this morning. A convenient time—friendless—morning, so calling to confirm his aloneness, his at-home-ness, his lack-of-male-comrade-ness, she headed optimistically toward his intermittent attentions, his thumped-upside-the-head affections, the focusing slap of his lover's touch, his willingness to jerk and grab her to his crushing chest, though she knew he did not like her for it.

At 8 a.m. Center Street was quiet as she biked in and out of the white lines. There was no reason for anyone to be there. At the post office she said hello to an old lover who was interested in how good she was looking but was married. She dropped five fat long envelopes into the mailbox.

"College applications to get my teaching credential," she replied when he asked.

He laughed, wiped at the oil stains on his jeans, and headed toward his old Plymouth. She waved goodbye then went to see Rick at 8:30 roommate vacancy time.

Despite his roommate whose return was anticipated like the Second Coming, anticipated but not easily calculated, they began undressing in the kitchen. Somewhere between the hellos and his incessant guitar playing, Rick removed their clothing quickly, making laundry piles on the linoleum.

Though his room waited vacant upstairs, they would fuck on the couch he indicated by placing her there. *How romantic,* she thought, the urgency of woven cords scraping her back, his ample weight dangling over her, the immediacy of the impending roommate, the five minutes of gripping dominance before he rolled off and went to the kitchen to put on his Levi's, leaving her still shaking amid the cushions.

Rick played a concert for one on his stereo, on his guitar, on his flute, on his harmonica. She curled next to his leg, stroking it in chords of silent frustration. She tried to imagine ways to make him be nice. It was easier to imagine herself leaving, but she had nowhere to go. Then the phone rang. It was someone calling for Rick's roommate, Eleanor gathered, as Rick explained the significance, justified the corporate pagan ritualness, of the Mormon mission his roommate was on today.

Rick's voice implied, "We men are discussing important things." It sounded like the men on the phone included God. When Rick got bored, his hand signals to Eleanor indicated, "You can wait while God and I wait for this guy to shut up."

Still involved with the phone, Rick stood by the open kitchen door and threw a butcher knife into the backyard fence. She ran to fetch it. He pointed it at her occasionally but mostly he heaved it end over end into the fence. It reminded her of softball. He was not very good at hitting the target. He was better at getting the knife from her before she had a chance to try it.

Bored with that, she began kissing his neck, occasionally slipping into his ear as he leaned against the wall. The roommate's friend was in one of Rick's ears, and her tongue was in the other, and God was in there. Rick tolerated this intrusion until he had a hard-on then he shoved her head down on it, friendly at first, then more insistent until his penis flattened deep in her throat making her gag, really gag, and before he could come, she pulled away, escaping from under his hand. She hid behind his back crying, no longer liking this kind of play.

One late spring evening Eleanor lay on her bed looking out the window thinking, *The old woman down the street in the green aluminum house is not dead,* though it had been years since Eleanor had seen her outside even to wave goodbye to her visiting son. He had been Jamie's best friend.

Eleanor watched the woman's husband watering the lawn, changing the sprinklers, and thought, *Poor man. His wife is dead. His stiffness is his hurt from it.* But his wife was not dead. Long ago they carried her down the hill in a screaming white smear, her heart lost within the nearly two hundred pounds of her. Embalmed, improved, they brought her back in their tan four-door. She sat in her house like a tomb. It rained. The sun set. Her husband washed the car. Eleanor wondered if she still sat in front of the TV in a brown plastic recliner, her back to a portrait done forty years ago.

"Who is she?" Eleanor had asked when she was ten, pointing at the amateurish oil painting of a woman who looked like a Miss Breck commercial—a thin soft rosy woman in white, a nurse with curly brown hair. "Where did you get that picture?" she had demanded, pulling her lint-flecked sweatshirt over her plump belly.

"Why that's Amanda, dear," the abundant woman had answered, smiling from within her powder puff cheeks.

"You? You looked like that?" Eleanor demanded again, swinging her ponytail over her shoulder to put the end in her mouth.

"Yes, dearie, that was Amanda."

Eleanor left taking what she could remember from the woman who lived in the house Jamie ran to nearly every day.

And not too long afterwards, the evening after Jamie's funeral, Amanda came to visit Eleanor's family. After they talked about the food and ate the ham and turkey and potato salad the neighbors had brought, Eleanor's father sent her to bed where she could hear Amanda talking.

"That Jamie, you should have seen him." There was a slapping sound as Amanda hit her thigh. "He loved that horn. Last Christmas, when he was with us, he played. He was smiling, that big smile. It made him so happy."

Eleanor had begun crying, seeing herself, a mixture of acne and fifth-grader, wanting to kiss Jamie goodbye as he left for a date. He was smiling and wearing shiny narrow shoes, tight narrow slacks, and a broad-chested white shirt. He looked like the boys all the big girls wanted, but she still wore her ponytail so severely pulled back it would dent her head forever. "Pretty is as pretty does," her disappointed mother would say when Eleanor came home from school crying because she had no friends.

Jamie's smile had slipped when Eleanor asked, "Could I please have a kiss?" And though her mother tried to make him, he would not. He shoved Eleanor against the wall as he tried to get out the kitchen door. Their mother grabbed him and tried to pull him back while Eleanor pressed herself against the wall and cried. She could remember that, but she could not remember him after that.

Then the abundant slow-moving Amanda came into Eleanor's bedroom and sat on the bed to comfort her. Eleanor looked into Amanda's rag-doll eyes poked into her generous face while Amanda cradled her and made her a story to go to sleep by. In the story Eleanor was a princess who rode white horses with her father, the king. She wore pink jewels in her hair, which her mother braided every morning, and she was so beautiful brave men kneeled to kiss her image. And her handsome noble brother was a prince who stood smiling stiffly outside her door, guarding her like his own future, and he loved her, and he did not go away.

But knowing the story was untrue, Eleanor had forgotten until now that Amanda had come to her and told it.

# PART TWO

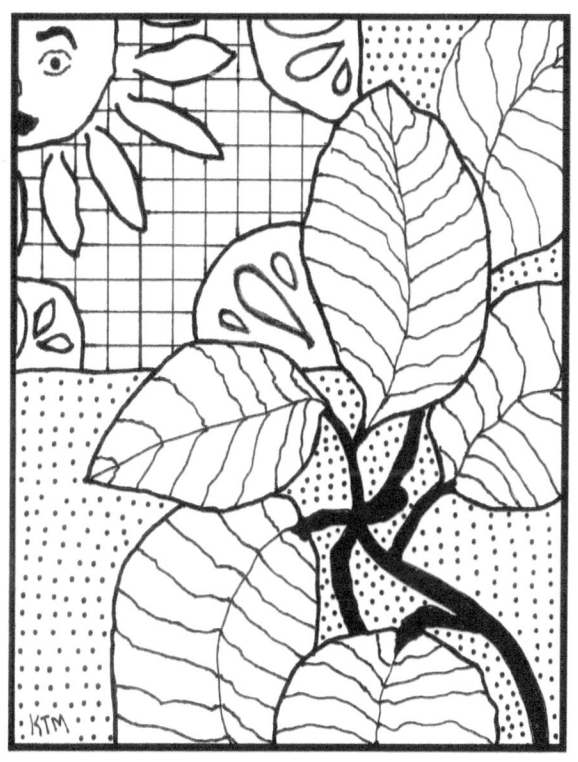

After another season lifeguarding, Eleanor arrived in southern Arizona to learn to be a grade school teacher. One Sunday sitting at her roommate's kitchen table waiting for her mother to call, she read a book about evolution. She was hoping to evolve—to become a scaled amphibian heading back toward the water or a bright yellow duck. She underlined, "Conforming to conventions leads to kangaroos." Kangaroos were dead ends in evolution. They hadn't been able to figure things out. Nothing new could come from them.

Eleanor believed in the book. "There's a right way to do everything," her mother said. If you didn't do things right you couldn't progress, but it was difficult to know what progress was. When he left home at eighteen, Jamie had become a dead end. The music he made came to a dead end. His car rolled over, slid, and was crushed. His saxophone was crushed. He no longer stood against the weight of his horn, no longer leaned back and played, tall, thin, and alone, his muscular arms tensed into the curve of the horn and the music.

The football players who lived in their house became dead ends too. Once they left the house, Eleanor never saw them again. She wanted to see farther, she wanted to see life continue outside the house, but she knew only that when they stopped being in the house, they had stopped and had become only mysteries. Their wives and children were part of the mysteries.

Now that she was away from home, she had become one of the mysteries. She felt full of suspense and confusion. She disappeared. She wanted to ask her mother how she should behave, but it had been a long time since her mother lived outside of the house. Her mother had been a petite blonde sorority girl, the kind who went to parties and kept men waiting in the lobby while she talked on the phone. She couldn't understand why Eleanor wasn't that way.

"I don't see why you can't make friends," her mother said. "Aren't you normal?"

Eleanor didn't know how to answer her. She couldn't say "Yes" or "No."

When she was lonely, she called home crying. Her mother would say, "Stop crying. You're being ridiculous." Her mother refused to see dead ends, voids.

Eleanor thought Teddy might also live in a void, far away from hers, on the other side of their mother, but she wasn't sure, and he wouldn't tell. After Jamie died, Teddy stopped talking to her. "Dial-a-Nile-movie-meter-remover" was all he would say. After Jamie was gone, Teddy was left alone with an uncontrollable bedroom that could only be cleaned when their mother broke through the door in a rampaging tantrum, trying to regain her control.

That was when Teddy had begun falling into Eleanor. When they passed in the hallway, he would press himself against the wall then lose his balance and fall, hitting the other wall with her, entangling himself with her instead of being separate and alone. That was how they had evolved, separate and alone.

Eleanor tried to listen to her mother. Perhaps if Jamie had listened, he would still be alive. Her mother said she shouldn't struggle so hard at school. She should have a good time or come back home. Her mother hadn't wanted Jamie ever to leave home. Eleanor wanted to go to her roommate Cynthia's room, lie on the floor of her closet, and bury herself in her pile of clothes, but she knew she shouldn't, not because Cynthia would mind, she probably wouldn't, but because it was a strange thing to do, and she was trying not to do strange things anymore. Cynthia's things smelled like Eleanor's mother's things—like powder and make-up and lotion—reminding Eleanor of being a little girl watching her mother dress, thinking her mother was perfect, and this made her feel confused.

Back home when she felt confused she would go into her bedroom, lean her forehead against her mirror, and cry, asking, "Who are you? Who are you?"

"You're crazy! That's all you are! You're crazy!" her mother would scream at her.

Eleanor began reading her book again. The author's theory was that even instinctual behavior could be changed. The bee naturally went into its hive head first, but when the experimenter stabbed it repeatedly from behind with a pin, it learned to turn around. This was progress, the author said.

When Eleanor got tired of reading, she went outside to her garden. She listened for the phone to ring while she pulled dead plants and stuffed them in a garbage sack as her father had taught her to do. If her mother called, maybe her father would say hello to her. He usually said hello to her.

Imagining her mother might visit, she looked at her garden in quadrants—tops and stems, left and right—as her mother would while talking about suitcase zippers and public bathrooms and distracting herself. The garden looked fine when Eleanor pictured it distorted that way; then, she noticed an absence of wrought iron and ornamental shrubbery in the two-by-twelve foot area surrounded by gravel and dirt.

"Can't you find anyone to do clipped shrubbery?" her mother

would ask. "We have two separate areas now, one for animal forms and one for natural shapes. I think you would like the new animal shapes. I think all the neighbors do."

The tomato vines were healthy but not producing enough to give away as her mother would want her to do if the garden was back home as her mother wanted it to be. "You don't seem to be using all of your tomatoes. I could find a use for all of those tomatoes," her mother would say. Eleanor knew what her mother would say because things between them were frozen into place long ago. She would have to unstick them if she was going to evolve.

Her mother would want to see mirrors. "Where's your bedroom mirror, dear? There doesn't seem to be a mirror in here. I couldn't find one in the living room either. Wouldn't you like a nice living room mirror?" She would walk through the apartment on her slim ivory heels in her straight ivory skirt and jacket.

But Eleanor didn't like mirrors. She looked too much like her dead brother.

"Your skin feels just like his," her mother said as she tucked Eleanor into bed the night he died.

"Do you cook for yourself very often?" her mother would ask as she turned over Cynthia's Mexican straw hot pads on the walls. She would be looking for mirrors.

"Do you cook for yourself very often?" her mother's letters said. They were friendly and hard evidence of her mother's good will: "We'd like to get you some wrought iron, dear, whenever you think you're ready for it. We like the black, but you might prefer the white, especially living in the desert, though if you moved home you would probably want black. We could call and order it for you and have it delivered, or we could wait until you decide to move back. Teddy brought the pieces for his front yard home himself, but he's doing his backyard now, and he had it delivered. You'll see it when you come home. We hope you'll be home soon. We love you, Mother."

Teddy was her brother, and Mother was her mother, Eleanor reminded herself as she pulled dead leaves off her tomato plants, her mother of twenty-three disjointed years. In her imagination the years looked like huge plains broken along fault lines, like random stacks of bricks mortared together, waiting throughout time to be built into something, into houses, into medieval city walls.

Eleanor was feeling better when her mother called that evening. She couldn't remember what she was going to say. It had something to do with her life and seemed important, but now that her mother was on the phone, it didn't.

"What have you been doing?" her mother asked.

"Nothing much."

"Well, why don't you get busy? We've had a busy day. We've been working in the garden."

"I have been too," she said, feeling guilty because her mother thought she had wasted her day.

"Your father accidentally chopped up your carnations though."

"My carnations? The ones I planted when I was a kid?"

"Yes, he was hoeing, and he didn't see them. I hope you don't mind."

"No, it's okay," she lied.

"Well, it just about killed me. I remember all the bouquets you used to bring me. You've always been such a sweet girl. I don't understand why things have been so hard for you."

"I don't know why either, Mother," she said, and for a moment she really didn't know.

"What a fun day it will be," Eleanor told the fourth-graders she was student teaching as they boarded the bus for a tour of the county fire station. She was relying on the power of suggestion. She put her hand on her stomach and tried to relax. She knew it wasn't normal to be frightened by a gang of firemen.

When they arrived, the children ran into the garage where the firemen lined them up. Eleanor helped. When her supervising teacher, Mrs. Rupert, finally got off the bus, Captain C. R. Byrd introduced himself and gave the orders. The children called him "Captain Whirlybird" and pointed at his walrus mustache. They wanted to know where Smokey Bear was. He told them they could have a plastic Smokey Bear if they were good. Commander Bob waved at them on his way to coffee.

All the firemen had mustaches and shaved necks, Eleanor noticed, white T-shirts, blue pants, and red suspenders. Their big shoulders, big forearms, and scrubbed-red skin reminded her of Fireman Rick, and her high school boyfriend, Andrew, and the football players she had grown up with.

As the firemen tossed the boys and girls into the firetruck, she thought of the football players, so many of them, having motorcycles, an affinity for wrestling, the ability to be more stimulating than junior high. There was Clint, chasing her around the backyard as he and Teddy threw darts, and Clint's younger brother, Chad, stealing the groceries from her as she carried them in for her mother, teasing her, blocking her way.

In the evening she and Michael wrestled in the living room. At school she showed off the bruises on her arms. They meant Michael liked her. He told her she was tough, which meant she was like the boys, and if she could be like the boys then her mother wouldn't be jealous of her and her father wouldn't be embarrassed by her.

In eighth grade she was sick one month. All day she was alone, but in the afternoons Danny came home and talked about the foxy girls on TV and the foxy girls at college. When her mother came home, she called in Danny to talk to her while she cooked. He told her how pretty she was and what a good cook she was. She gave him food and hugs and told him thank you.

One afternoon when her mother was gone and Danny was home, Eleanor lay on the couch feeling awful. Her heart was pounding, and she was breathing hard and shaking. When he came over to her, her heart pounded faster, her breathing got harder, and she shook more. She wanted him to hold her and make her feel better. He put his hand on her forehead.

"What's wrong with you?" he asked.

She couldn't tell him what was wrong, but she always felt this way when he was around. She wanted to tell him it would go away, but then he would go away, and she liked him putting his hand on her forehead and on her arm. She wanted him to lie down beside her, but she knew that was what her mother didn't want him to do, so she turned over in her blanket, and he went away.

At the fire station she was afraid she would start shaking because she was afraid the firemen wouldn't like her, and if they did like her there would be trouble and she wouldn't know what to do. She wished everything didn't remind her of something that had happened long ago.

She watched as the firemen loaded Mrs. Rupert into the truck, pulling on her arms and pushing from behind. Mrs. Rupert called over the firemen standing with Eleanor and made them get into the truck to help. When Mrs. Rupert was settled, she had one fireman sitting on either side of her and the children alone in the back of the truck.

Mrs. Rupert reminded Eleanor of her mother though they were so different. Her mother played bridge and went to plays in L.A. Still, there was something. Perhaps it was the way Mrs. Rupert acted around the firemen. Her mother would like the firemen too. Her mother liked Eleanor's boyfriends, sometimes more than Eleanor did.

In high school when Eleanor met Andrew, her parents hadn't wanted her to go out with him even though he was big, 6'6", and played college football. They thought she was lying when she told them he liked her, but after she convinced them it was true, he and her mother became friends. They sat on the couch watching TV, waiting for her to come home, then took turns yelling at her. They wanted her in the house, they said. This was because they loved her, they said. She would look toward her bedroom door, wishing she were behind it; then, she and Andrew would go into the living room and have sex. Andrew liked having sex, so she acted like she did, and he would tell her he loved her. She loved him, too, sometimes, but not while having her head forced against the wall in quick deep thuds.

After Andrew left, her mother would ground her. "He can come here, but I don't want you going anywhere with him."

As the children came and went, Captain Whirlybird gave tours of the bathroom and dormitories so they could see how firemen lived. Firemen lived like sardines, Eleanor thought. When

*Toy*

she was left alone in the dormitory with the firemen, they looked at her expectantly. It was awkward and confusing thinking of what they might want. She wanted to be twelve again so she could give them brownies and watch them, but she knew they would think it strange if she, a young school teacher, silently handed them brownies then wouldn't talk to them, would only watch.

They liked her dress and her tan, they said. Hardly any girls wore dresses anymore.

"Where are you from?" they asked.

"Rio Grande Grade School."

"We know, but are you from around here?"

"No. I live with my roommate and her plant on the other side of town."

She knew she wasn't giving them the answers they wanted.

Leonard, one of the students, pulled Eleanor's sleeve. He wanted to tell a joke. He asked why firemen wore red suspenders.

"I don't know."

"To hold their pants up," Leonard said, pushing her arm and running away.

She giggled as the firemen smiled at each other and snapped their red suspenders.

When everyone got back, Captain Whirlybird took them through the rest of the station. There were two kitchens and two dining rooms, so during emergencies two crews could cook and eat at the same time; then, there was a TV room, a study room, and a weight lifting room to go to before and after eating.

It was like a mad cook's dream, Eleanor thought, picturing the men coming in, big and hungry, their shoulders rolling forward, their white T-shirts linked, rows of curving white T-shirts entering together, eating together, going back to work together.

Staring at the giant pots and spoons hanging on the walls, she backed into the corner, put one hand against her mouth, the other against her stomach, and hoped the pain would go away. She thought of Andrew, with his big chest and shoulders, pinning her against the wall when they had sex standing up and of having her tonsils out and of having sex on the couch. She couldn't talk or swallow, so she shut her eyes and hid her face in the cushions, crying, tasting blood, and waiting for the sex to end.

She knew it wasn't right to think of these things now. She could never figure out if she'd had a normal life and had just reacted strangely to it or not. She had come from a nice family, that's what her mother said. Maybe someday she would be able to calm down and behave. She took her fingers out of her mouth.

Captain Whirlybird led them outside for the bucket brigade next. His shift, Shift One, had a neat stack of official metal pails that went with the official dump tank. Shift One was the official championship bucket brigade team for Arizona, he said proudly as he showed the newspaper clippings of his boys.

He did the timing, and Commander Bob shouted "Go!" and "Stop!" The firemen passed bucket after bucket, slopping water over themselves, slapping their wet pants, and smiling at their tennis shoes. The children laughed.

Then they let the kids try. Leonard wanted to be commander, so they let him shout, "Go!" and "Stop!" Everyone got to pass one bucket. That was enough, the children said, shaking out their red arms and rubbing their red hands. None of them wanted to get wet.

While Mrs. Rupert gathered the boys and girls, counting their heads, the firemen let Eleanor try. They put her in the middle to cover her mistakes, but she didn't make many. The firemen were so impressed they invited her back for coffee.

"Any time in the morning or afternoon. We're free just about all the time."

They gave her a little card with their work schedule. She stared at their card and mustaches, suspenders, and tennis shoes and told them "Maybe" though she thought not.

To end the tour, the firemen wanted to show how much water the big truck put out. Commander Bob held the stopwatch to time the maneuver. Captain Whirlybird stood at one end of the truck and Fireman Don, who was older, at the other.

Leonard said, "Go!"

Fireman Don and Captain Whirlybird peeled off the hose. Fireman Kent, who was young and cute, ran holding the end. The captain turned the dials. When the water finally came, Fireman Kent looked at Eleanor while he made arcs and circles with the spray, and everyone pointed at the rainbows.

Fireman Kent was making a big wave when suddenly the stream of water became a trickle. Leonard had twisted the dials as Captain Whirlybird had done and shut the water off. Eleanor apologized and gathered the children. Commander Bob went to get the Smokey Bear. Mrs. Rupert took Leonard by the hand. Fireman Kent stood sadly in the mud with his limp dripping hose as Eleanor waved goodbye.

One evening Eleanor left her living room; her new boyfriend, Paul; her roommate, Cynthia; and the TV to look at the philodendron on the kitchen table. Even though it was Cynthia's, she felt they were friends. She wanted to take a picture of it, but her Polaroid was out of film. She got her drawing pad and numbered pencils to draw it instead. With various shades of gray, she rendered the dark greens, the light greens, the shadows of the philodendron exactly.

While Eleanor enjoyed shading each leaf, trying to make it pliant, Paul and Cynthia began talking, turned off the TV, got out their guitars, and sang Spanish love songs. Cynthia, with her greasy dark hair and large breasts, studied Spanish and loved Hispanic culture. She liked to click her fingers and kick up her black leather pumps, trying to reach the drooping pears of her rear end with her heels.

Eleanor began another drawing. Instead of Cynthia's Mexican straw hot pads and leather paintings, sprigs of ivy—short, nearly bare sprigs—came out of the walls very thinly. Eleanor would like running her hands through them—the way they flapped when she did and for a long time after. She imagined one day while Cynthia spread jelly on the table and her toast, the ivy vines, with their infinite power to grow and struggle and push ahead, would wrap themselves around Cynthia's throat as she ate piece after piece of toast, and when the jelly was gone, Cynthia would be trapped at the table with nothing but dry bread.

Then Paul and Cynthia said they were hungry. They wanted popcorn and chips and Pepsi. Eleanor offered to go to the store. It was only a few blocks. She could walk. Paul told her to get dog food for his dog and plant food for the plant. There was a special on dog food at her store, he had read in the paper. It would be foolish for him to get it at his store. And the plant was probably lacking nitrogen. No amount of attention would improve it until the essential elements were replaced in the soil.

Because Eleanor lived on the desert, when she went on walks this was what she did: look for houses with lawns in front. When she found one, she stopped and waved her hands—*swish, swish*—

over the grass. It flapped when she did and was wet and green. Often, like tonight, a dog would begin barking, and, not wanting anyone to see what she had done, she would leave.

At the store she felt like a rodeo cowboy in her baggy butt overalls as she maneuvered her shopping cart down the aisles. "What are you looking for?" her mother would ask rhetorically. *Plant food—where the hell's the plant food?* She found the plant food, the dog food, the popcorn, the chips, and the Pepsi then stared at the plants growing under the fluorescent lights and packages of seeds.

At the checkout stand she watched an old woman crowd into the line behind hers. The woman looked up with a grin that pulled apart wrinkles like drapes across a window as she shook an apple at the cashier who refused to see.

"Hee, hee, hee. Here, here—my apple. Got an apple," the old woman said and laid out a dime from the hollowness of her soft frayed coin purse.

The clerk shuffled through the charts to find the cost. "Five and two-thirds ounces—baking apple," she read from the plastic card.

"What's price?" the old woman cried out. "What's price?"

Eleanor could see the lines of the woman's face stretch all the way down her neck. She envied her. All she needed was an apple. Eleanor would be glad when she was old and wrinkled and didn't have to be concerned with anyone anymore. She wouldn't be expected to be.

"I'm not going to bake it, I'm just going to eat it," the old woman confided to her hand as she flashed her dime around.

"That will be thirty-five cents," the checker punched out.

The old woman shouted, "Dime! Only have dime!"

The checker tried to take the apple. The old woman would not let go.

As Eleanor looked at her change, confused by the possibilities, she saw a man in line behind the old woman slip the checker a quarter.

"Ee, ee," the old woman said as the checker handed the apple to her, and Eleanor was pleased that this too might be the ending of her future.

Walking home, Eleanor studied an ad for bedding plants. They were going for a price she could afford. But if she bought the plants, if she planted the plants, she couldn't go home at Christmas or they would be lying dead at her doorstep. Cynthia wouldn't do watering; it gave her sun poisoning, she said.

When Eleanor realized this, she hurried home to draw more ivy for the kitchen walls because she wanted very much to go home to the ocean, to stand alone in the space between the rock cliffs and cold crashing water. There would be trees and soft flowering bushes, and the water would be thick enough to hang in the air. At the beach there would be fog, and if she reached her arms out far enough, she could wave her hands and not see them swish anything at all.

*I'm learning to cooperate with tribal medicine*, Eleanor told herself as she sliced her third zucchini for the casserole she was taking to Paul's potluck, *and I am feeling better for it. I am learning to make friends with my enemy, the stomach. The lesson of tribal medicine has been a hard one, but it has brought me to an understanding of white bread, the food of my youth. I can now apologize for the mistakes I made prior to my understanding.*

Then she took what tribal medicine had prescribed: the little white pills. If she took them when she first got up, she fell back asleep, but if she didn't take them soon enough they didn't do any good. When the pills were really working, no matter how much water she drank, her dry tongue stuck to her mouth, and when she stood up she saw only black behind her wide-staring eyes. These were some side benefits of tribal medicine, the doctor had explained. Tribal medicine helped her get through the day.

Whenever her mother called, she asked about the developments in tribal medicine. Tribal medicine was expensive, Eleanor said. But well worthwhile, her mother replied. Her mother was impressed with tribal medicine: "I bet you like being on tranquilizers," she said. Her mother would like her doctor of tribal medicine, his kindly tone, his patience, the way he wrote prescriptions with such authority, Eleanor knew. Whenever Eleanor expressed doubts about tribal medicine, her mother said, "We must do whatever the doctor says, dear. He knows more than we ever could." Eleanor was learning to express confidence in tribal medicine. It was easier to accept that way. By accepting tribal medicine she felt better, more calm.

A few weeks before when Eleanor flew home for Christmas, her stomach hurt so much she asked her mother to take her to the doctor. He ordered fasting and barium, examinations and tests. It was lonely staying in the house all day. She couldn't make her mother stay home—she didn't know how. She was embarrassed to call anyone—she didn't have anything to say. She felt like an octopus collapsed and drying out on the recliner. She knew it made her mother feel guilty to come home, all colorful and smiling, and find her that way.

"Is something wrong?" her mother asked as they drove home from the last test.

"I know I shouldn't be, but I'm so unhappy. I'm so bored and lonely."

"Well, what do you want me to do about it?" her mother asked.

"Nothing. It's fine. Everything's fine."

"If you were a grown-up woman with a family of your own, you'd be in trouble. You'd have to take care of everybody. What do you expect from me! What do you want me to do?" Her mother's creamy pink face had dark holes at the mouth and nose when she yelled.

Eleanor regretted making her mother unhappy. She moved closer to the car door, but that didn't please her mother either.

"I had a wonderful vacation planned for you. And now you're sick. I don't know what you want from me! After all, it *is* Christmas!"

She asked her mother to stop yelling.

"Well, you're just trying to make me feel guilty, and I don't. Is it my fault you're sick? Am I the one to blame?"

She asked her mother to be quiet. She asked calmly and politely and by screaming. But her mother had a lot to say.

"I'm sick of feeling guilty," her mother said with clenched teeth. "Now, if you can't keep yourself entertained, I don't know what you want me to do. Your father and I have *commitments*."

Eleanor asked her mother to stop the car. She told her mother she would like to get out. Her mother stopped the car. Eleanor got out. The big powerful engine of her mother's big red car ground out black smoke and left her behind. Eleanor wished it wasn't so easy to make her mother feel guilty.

It was somewhat embarrassing holding her stomach and crying as she walked the hill home. It was early evening, and her father would be home from work. Perhaps he would be surprised when her mother came home from the hospital without her and would inquire about her. She was only a mile from their house. If her father came looking for her, he would find her.

As she walked, she thought about Jamie. Her parents wouldn't let something happen to her too. They had suffered enough because of Jamie, they had told her. She and Teddy weren't to do anything that would make them suffer more.

She could not remember the last time Jamie left the house. *Running away from home* was how she thought of it. He was going to play music. Their parents hadn't wanted him to go. Perhaps their mother had waved goodbye, smiling and hugging him, but Eleanor didn't know, and now she was afraid to ask. She didn't remember a fight, but there could have been a fight. There could have been no fight, and he could have been running away from home just the same. There could have been silence the night before as he packed, the day he left. Her parents were silent about showing him the way, and he was lost and confused and went off a cliff and died.

There was a map, but it was still at home. She had overheard her father talking about it after the funeral. He felt guilty for not showing Jamie the way. Years later, she had driven the same winding road one night. She was tired, and the shadows of her headlights on the mountains got confusing, and she almost followed the bright lights into the mountain wall.

When she walked into the house, she was surprised to find her mother and father watching TV. They didn't care to speak to her then, but later, when she wouldn't come out of her room, her mother wanted to speak to her very much. Her mother pounded on her door and said, "Let me in here! I'm your mother!"

On Christmas, Eleanor felt awkward exchanging presents. Because no one mentioned what her mother did, Eleanor wondered if anything had happened at all. So many things had gone unmentioned, she could not be sure what parts of her life were real. She thought the experiences she shared with her family should be real, but the experiences they agreed to share were never the ones she remembered most.

When she finished the casserole, she decided to write her old college art teacher. He used to listen to her when she talked to him. She felt she owed him something for that, but he insisted there was nothing she could give.

"Hello," she wrote. "I am sorry about my last note to you. Of course, you could not reply. I am writing to apologize. I was somewhat depressed by the decisions of tribal medicine. Tribal medicine had dictated for me a diet of French fries and white bread, supplemented by drugs. It was the white bread, really, that brought on the depression. I read an article about it. My stomach is better now. I'm learning how to control it. I'm making hors d' oeuvres for twelve, sausage quiche. It's all in the oven now."

It wasn't, but how was he to know.

"I'm writing to say I'm happy and not depressed anymore even though I am still eating white bread. I'm eating more French fries now, and the saturated fats in the cooking oil, when brought to the extremely high temperature necessary to denature potatoes, are counteracting the depression brought on by the white bread. Really. I read an article on it."

She paused, considering the effect of Cynthia's dirty dinner plate on the boldly patterned living room carpet.

"I am writing not only to apologize, but to offer you the combination that will unleash the ringing sound inside my telephone. You forgot, I am sure, to ask for it. You are forgetting also, I am sure, to ask when I am coming to visit. Unfortunately, I am tied to my supply of French fries and white bread and will not be coming soon."

She wished she had a French fry to suck on to relieve her anxiety. She finished writing, then went to the bathroom taking Cynthia's curlers and mirror from the kitchen table. She enjoyed lining up the curlers according to color around the base of the toilet.

As she graded her fourth-graders' homework at the kitchen table, Eleanor imagined Paul getting up and washing his Mustang, buffing the narrow pirouettes of the pinstripes on the bright orange hood with her yellow sweatshirt, the slim angular neatness of his body professional and controlled. Once the interior was reupholstered, he would sell the Mustang at a big profit, he told her. Because he worked hard on it every weekend, she knew.

Thinking about Paul made her think about her mother, and thinking about her mother made her think about ice cream. Unfortunately, she was always thinking. She began writing a story about ice cream. Maybe she would read it to her fourth graders.

*Once upon a time a fat girl named Eloise sat in front of the TV watching* Days of Our Lives *and eating ice cream. She was a fat girl because of eating ice cream and watching TV, but she didn't know what else to do. Sometimes the fat girl's mother came in and watched her. Her mother liked watching her better than watching TV, especially if the girl did something bad, if she chewed on her* toes or turned off the TV. *The fat girl's mother was blonde and small and never did anything bad.*

*One day the fat girl said to her mother, "Mother, please don't bring home any more ice cream."*

*But the mother swelled up like a giant amoeba ready to engulf the fat girl. Skin flapped from the mother's arms, and she became a huge bat-like thing.*

*"But I might want some," the bat-mother said. "Sometimes I want some. I don't always eat any, but I want to know we have some."*

*The bat-mother wrote "ICE CREAM" on her shopping list in giant curlicue letters. The skin attached from her arms to her legs flapped and dangled ungracefully.*

*The bat-mother brought home half-gallons of spumoni and chocolate, two half gallons at a time now, for variety. It was a lovely thing to do, all the bat-mother's friends said. The bat-mother stood in the kitchen and looked at the fat girl watching* Days of Our Lives *and eating ice cream.*

*"I'm worried about you," the bat-mother said, her pink skin folding around her. "Why don't you stop that? Isn't it boring?"*

Eleanor remembered sometimes for company Mother brought out three half gallons of ice cream on a silver tray. The candlelight twinkled her pale blonde hair silver and gold. "Ooohh" and "Aaahh," the company said. Mother ate one spoonful from her bowl while the company watched.

"Why don't you do like I do," she said to Eleanor.

Eleanor put the end of her braid in her mouth and watched. Mother never ate another spoonful as long as Eleanor watched. Eleanor's handsome father sat at the head of the table and refused to watch.

One day in high school Eleanor watched as the spoonfuls of ice cream she fed to the garbage disposal swirled down the sink. A spoonful for Eleanor, one for the sink, until the half-gallon was gone; then, she took half a chocolate cake, sliced it neatly, and pushed part of each slice into her face and part into the sink, grabbing at bits of icing as they slid toward the drain. She ate them slippery and warm from the running water.

"Did you see the cake I left out? Did you eat the rest of it?" Mother asked when she came home.

"Yes, Mother. It was delicious."

"I'm glad you liked it. I made it for you."

Then Paul called. She read him the story about the bat-mother, the girl, and the ice cream. He said bats didn't eat ice cream. She thanked him. He told her more about bats. She thanked him again. Paul was so interesting, but while he was talking she started grading again. He told her about the people who would be at the party.

"Jim is an inventory analyzer."

"What does an inventory analyzer do?"

"That would be a good question to ask him."

"Okay. Thank you. Do you think anyone would be interested in hearing about tribal medicine?"

"Don't be silly like that. I have to work with these people."

Paul insisted she call things by their proper names, but sometimes it was hard for her to know what the proper names for things were.

After Paul hung up, she thought she was angry but decided it was better to feel positive. She couldn't really expect anyone to want to know what she was learning.

Cynthia came into the kitchen to make popcorn. She and her

tall bland boyfriend, Konrad, were relaxing after church. While Cynthia got out a clean saucepan instead of washing a dirty one, Eleanor watched Cynthia's breasts swinging freely inside her bathrobe. She recalled Cynthia standing at her bedroom mirror, lifting up parts of her body—breasts, stomach, thighs—to tell her what Konrad loved about them.

"I just like butter on mine," Cynthia said, "but Konrad likes a little Tabasco. I think Paul likes Tabasco too. Isn't that what Paul likes? You should ask Paul what he likes."

Eleanor looked up from grading. "Paul isn't here. I don't know what he likes."

Cynthia looked at her. "Well, Konrad likes Tabasco, and I was just asking."

"I'm sorry."

"That's all right. I know you and Paul aren't as close as Konrad and I are."

Cynthia dumped the popcorn into a bowl and onto the floor, then stirred in butter and Tabasco. More popcorn flew out. Konrad came in. He and his dirty dishwater blond hair towered over Cynthia's short round figure. Eleanor stared at his hand as he reached for the Tabasco and knocked more popcorn on the floor. He and Cynthia crunched on it as they kissed.

"Come on, little momma," he said to Cynthia. They went to watch TV.

Eleanor stared at the flattened gray popcorn on the floor. She pulled out another piece of paper and thought of another story to write. It was called "Diversionary Tactics." In it the girl got her way.

It was nearly three o'clock when Eleanor wrapped the zucchini casserole in a bath towel and put it in the back seat of her little car. Paul didn't want to take the Mustang. He was afraid it would get dirty.

At the party there was lots of food. Everyone talked about it. "Look at all the food," they said. Eleanor took her pills so she could eat her white bread later. She couldn't eat anything now. At the party the guys watched TV, and the girls stood in the kitchen. In high school when Eleanor went to the college football players' parties, the guys stayed in the kitchen with the girls. The guys stood over the sink, opened the bottom of a beer can with an opener, turned the can over, and popped the top so all the beer shot into their mouths. When the girls tried it, the beer ran out of their mouths, and they ran outside and puked. But they were all more mature now.

Before they could eat, the girls had to finish their cooking, and after they ate, the girls washed their pans so they could take them home. Because she was too hungry to stay in the kitchen, Eleanor went in front of the TV with the guys. She fell asleep before dinner and Paul forgot to wake her up after, so she had to take her pan home dirty.

Before she went to sleep, she read a magazine story about a woman going insane. What she did was cook. There were recipes in the story, and Eleanor tore them out. At the end, the woman told her psychiatrist, "I control the cooking in my family, and my power is enormous." Eleanor laughed.

When Eleanor went to bed, the only way she could sleep

was to put her hand in her crotch. It rounded her out, she felt. After she arranged the ribbons down the front of her nightgown and across the bed, she folded her nightgown into a place for her hand between her legs. When the chuckling in the living room stopped and Paul came to bed, she turned her back to his crotch.

In the morning, after she repacked her night things and straightened the bed and the long white dog hairs on it, she went home. Her impression of going home was this: trash. Today the kitchen garbage can was in the bathtub. Cynthia had put it there, underneath the faucet, on Friday. It was Sunday. Eleanor took the trash can back to the kitchen then took a shower. She walked out of the bathroom, thinking her name should be "Chinaberry" today, something round and wrinkling.

In her room she found two postcards from her mother who loved her from Hawaii; a note from a friend who enclosed the Zippy comics, ticket stubs, and mustache hairs he thought she needed; and a letter written from a purple slush of diarrhea. That's what it said: "I was driving up north when I was attacked by a purple slush of diarrhea." It was signed by the father of her old best friend. She put the mail inside a green Saks Fifth Avenue bag her mother had given her.

She got out her textbook and class notes to write a lesson plan. "Eleanor Honoria Lihte: Sentence Structure for Fourth Graders" she typed then lay on her bed. The friend wanted to tell her about Devo Teddy Bear he said right before he signed, "Love." Eleanor didn't know what he meant. She put her hand in her crotch to reread his letter. It made her feel round.

She couldn't sleep now without her hand in her crotch, even though it was embarrassing, rolling over, bringing out the hand, red and crushed, when Cynthia opened her door, peeped in at her napping. Cynthia would look at the red hand as it lay hot on the pillow, then tried to support her or be useful, to indicate things, answer questions.

If Cynthia came in today holding a pan of burnt spaghetti or a torn bra, the red hand would point and say, "I took the trash can out of the bathroom. It's back in the kitchen now. It's empty. It's ready. I'm sorry. I wanted to shower." It would be a slapping hot fish: fingers stuck together into a solid slapping body, red scales, red layers inside.

Eleanor slept and dreamt she was standing at her green lab table in high school science. Everyone was given a small ordinary fish, but she got a chunk, seven inches long, of a big red fish placed in her hand. As the others examined their fish, she measured her section noting it was four inches thick. She wrote and they wrote the external dimensions of their fish. They searched and she searched for the line of digestive organs running through their fish. She filled out her study sheet realizing the others could know, but she could not know, what was on either side of a fish.

Then she became a fish swimming in a snow-melt lake. People cheered as she swam past then farther out until they stopped watching. She was swimming fast, faster than she ever had, but then she stopped swimming. She was still going fast toward the rocks and fallen trees that dammed the lake before it fell over the edge and became a river. She tried swimming strongly away from the trees and could not. She realized, though, if she stayed calm and kept swimming, it was peaceful in the little noises of the cold water, and she felt strong.

In the dream someone took the fish and lifted it. He stroked the fish, chuckling, and the fish turned round and wrinkled into a ball. Inside the ball in a dark space shaped by deep wrinkles were the secrets of the fish, and the fish would not be a fish—it would not lay flat and open in the hand. It wrinkled around itself like a bug hiding its soft underside.

Eleanor woke up remembering in kindergarten during nap time lying by the open schoolroom door. Little flat bugs walked by, and she stroked them into balls and kept them until recess when she put them back under the ivy where they could hide away.

One Saturday during Paul's business stay in San Francisco, Eleanor sat at Cynthia's kitchen table studying the postcard from the cave he had visited, "The World Famous Chinese Meat Locker." Stalactites and stalagmites zigzagged up and down like giant teeth. It reminded her of a kid from lifeguarding last summer, of his big crooked teeth when he smiled. He was small for his age, and when the big boy who protected him went on vacation, the other kids ganged up on him at the park and pushed him down. His head hit a spigot, and he died. When the big boy came back, he didn't have his little friend anymore.

In the card Paul asked her to send pictures of his Mustang. He missed it, he said. She thought of him sitting on his motel bed alone, without his Mustang, dressed in a neat white shirt and dark slacks like Jamie had worn. If the maid came in she would be distracted by Paul's thin muscular presence and not able to clean the room. Paul would be unaware of her discomfort and the effect of his thin muscular presence. When the maid left quietly without doing her work, he would think nothing of it. He would press his hands onto his thighs then buff his shoes and pretend not to be bored. In college before, Eleanor would cut off her hair when she was bored.

She walked outside to take Polaroid pictures of the Mustang. The perspectives were interesting, and there were no people interfering with the sensual lines of the car. Paul would like that.

Weaving the Mustang in and out of traffic on her way to the college pool, she loved the warmth of the black leather upholstery and the identity of her purple sunglasses. It was good to be where she knew no one, where she wasn't looking for guys to pick up, where no one was watching her and reporting her to her mother.

At a stoplight she saw a billboard for the Cosmic Search band—five guys wearing torn T-shirts and worn jeans with black leather jackets and white leather high-tops, untied. Their hair was shaved and dyed purple like her sunglasses and orange like the Mustang. She wished she looked like them, tough but vulnerable, her jeans baggy at the crotch. The guy in the car next to her smiled, and she revved her engine. When the light changed, she got away first, but then he wasn't there to look at.

In the locker room as she undressed, she noticed two women in the big gang shower. They were short and round and had their arms locked around each other in a close embrace, but they were kicking each other and trying to throw each other down.

"Stop it!" Eleanor yelled.

"Leave us alone!" they yelled.

"Someone is going to get hurt!"

"No one is going to get hurt!" They stood holding each other to show this was true.

Eleanor left the locker room hearing the slap of flesh against flesh and against tile. She was glad she wasn't the lifeguard having to tell them what to do. It was so hard to know how to make them.

As she swam, making the long smooth pull down the center of her body, she saw herself grabbing a gold horse's mane with her left hand and being able to swing her right leg over and up onto the horse. She wondered why she saw herself doing that, then remembered she used to do it all the time. She could ride her beautiful Palomino backwards and could hang off the side, reaching down to lift the rein off the ground even if her horse was galloping, and could ride with no bridle at all, just swing on and go. She wondered what people would think now if they saw her swing on a horse and go. They would probably think it childish, her enthusiasm for horses, but she had felt so grown up then.

She had been so confident of the tiny white stars she had embroidered on the blue field of her horse's blanket. And so confident she could save her horse some way after she had rolled playfully in the arena then hooked her back shoe in the chain-link fence. She had saved her, with the help of the other children, though she died later when her father took her to a mountain pasture where the wild animals outran her. Eleanor had tried to stop him, but she couldn't, so she had forgotten those days instead.

That was after Jamie died. Her parents had not been able to save him either. Though they visited him in the hospital every day, their care was useless. Later her mother told her it was best he had died. Eleanor didn't think so, but she no longer felt sure. The confidence she had felt guiding her horse through the fields, moving her with the pressure of her knees or the angle of her body, began to drift away. She had moved back inside the house, wanting to stay there more and more.


Back home at the kitchen table, Eleanor ate Tru Blu vanilla cookies and watched Cynthia and Konrad as they played *Love Boat* on the couch in front of the TV. Konrad lay down, pretending he was the ship, while Cynthia kneeled over him, steering.

Eleanor was glad Paul wasn't watching as she dangled cookies from her ears, puckered her face into the parody of a sour cynical look, and chatted silently with Cynthia's plant. She laughed and was happy with the plant.

During snack time at school she put food in her ears and made faces behind Mrs. Rupert's back, making the children laugh. Once Mr. Mack, the principal, caught her. She thought he wanted to laugh, but he couldn't afford to in front of Mrs. Rupert: She wouldn't make herself diminutive and twist her head up to look at him and smile when he talked. After that Eleanor tried to make life easier for him. She took over the class when he came into the room, so he could take Mrs. Rupert into the cloakroom to praise her.

Eleanor was glad she and Paul kept their lives separate, each one working toward some other goal. When they ate out, each paid exactly half. She was proud to be able to afford half of Paul's bar tab. They had decided the correct number of nights she should sleep over: one during the weekend and one during the week, allowing them the proper closeness—and the proper distance too.

Eleanor looked at her pictures of the Mustang. On one she drew a girl waving. She put frizzy hair on the girl, turned her into a clown, wrote, "Hi from Eleanor." She wanted to send it to Paul, but he wouldn't like it. She would have to throw it away. Instead she taped it to the refrigerator and threw the rest away. When Paul came home, he would have his Mustang again.

The next Saturday after Eleanor finished grading her students' homework, she decided to play "From India." She wanted to be like the young woman from India in her class who was always correcting people. The woman was very sophisticated. She had been trained to feel superior.

"In our culture we don't see things that way," she said. "In the Indian culture we are not afraid to make distinctions as you Americans are. You are afraid to make judgments. You like only things that are unsophisticated, boring." When the students got angry, she replied, "I can criticize your culture. I am willing to criticize my own."

Eleanor decided to go criticize her own culture. She would go downtown to hate other people's gauze floral clothes the way the woman did. But she wouldn't say anything. That wouldn't be nice. That would be rude.

When Eleanor felt depressed she said to herself, "I can do many things: Be nice. Be sophisticated." She was nice. "Thank you," she said when she handed Paul's keys back whenever she picked him up at the airport. When people called for Cynthia and Eleanor got tired of talking to them, she dropped the receiver politely on the bed and went to the bathroom to wash her hot face and straighten the towels.

When she wanted to be rude, she played "Demented." It was her favorite game. When she played "Demented," she acted like Mrs. Rupert. She held an imaginary student firmly in her hands and said, "You're a bad boy, a bad, bad boy; but that's all right" and smiled very hard.

Mrs. Rupert liked to play "Demented" too. She would make Eleanor put a bad grade on a student's paper. When the student complained, Mrs. Rupert would make Eleanor change it. When Mr. Mack stopped in, Mrs. Rupert would tell him how much she trusted Eleanor, and they would go have coffee. When they got back, Mrs. Rupert would finish the game. She would collect the work Eleanor had assigned and throw it away. Mrs. Rupert was teaching her many things, if only she would learn.

Eleanor went into the kitchen, reshuffled the dirty dishes, and stuck out her tongue while she shook her grapefruit rind at Cynthia's velvet pictures of mountains and moons. She threatened them with the damp threads of her grapefruit. She practiced being from India.

Then she drove Paul's Mustang downtown, not shifting after the lights, playing "Automatic Mustang." It was a terrible thing to do to the clutch, Paul had said. At the stoplight, she put the car in neutral and played "Red Light, Green Light" with the accelerator. Growing up, she and Teddy played it with their milk: "Red light," Engineer Bill said, and they put their glasses down. "Green light," and they picked them up again.

"Red light, green light," Eleanor said as she pumped on the gas.

As she waited, she noticed the car on her right. She thought the young woman from India would say it was boring, was always doing the same thing, was unsophisticated, so she began making remarks about it.

Twisting the radio off, she said, "Cars." Then louder and to the right she said, "You car, you do the same things all the time." She told the control panel, "Same stupid cars! You're all stupid!"

She rolled down the window. Her mouth became a hoop. Words sprayed through it and onto the hoods of the cars. Her mouth became a high-pressure nozzle. Her body became a hose pumping out examples of stupid behavior.

"Honking!" she sprayed. "Hitting door panels in parking lots! Rear-end damage! Front wheel misalignment!" she blasted.

She imagined the wet cars honking, bumping bumpers, their plastic decals curling in the steam and the heat.

"Electric rear window defoggers! Seat belt buzzers!" she cried.

It was green light, but she couldn't hear what Engineer Bill said. Pushing hard on the "f" she said, "You *foolish* men!" to the Marenda County Rescue Squad. Eleanor Honoria Lihte was rude.


The day after graduation Eleanor was depressed, but she didn't know why. She was a teacher now, an adult, certified, grades K through twelve. Paul was taking her to dinner, all her work was done, she wasn't even alone: Cynthia and Konrad were in the kitchen cooking. But her thoughts kept escaping, and she knew it was a bad sign. She decided the only thing that could make her feel better and enjoy this day was chocolate.

She walked to the store and bought a large can of fudge sauce. She was impressed by its number of calories, more than a person needed for days. She wondered if they sent fudge sauce to starving children in Africa. A large can had more calories than quite a large amount of powdered milk.

Back at her apartment, Eleanor sat in front of the TV with the fudge sauce trying to be brain dead. It depressed her to think of going home. Her image of herself outside the house shimmered like the remains of an astronaut caught in space. But her mother's phone calls were more insistent now that she had no real reason to be away. She knew if she told her mother she didn't want to come home, her mother would say "All right," but then her mother would hang up.

Eleanor was afraid to return to her tiny homeland, the world of limited possibilities she knew. She might marry and raise children there, watch them grow and develop, then turn on them, begin ungrowing them, slowly pulling off the pieces that had been created until, wingless and blind, all the generations stumbled through the house together. Returning home would not be a wise choice.

Perhaps if she could get a job that would give her something. Perhaps a regular paycheck would give her something. She had never lived on one.

Then someone called inviting Cynthia and Konrad for drinks. They asked Eleanor to watch the beans they had been cooking all day. "Why not?" she said. She was in a stupor from the fudge sauce. She thought of all the things her speeding brain wanted her to do right then, but the beans and her stomach had her ground down between the TV and the stove.

It had been wonderful to graduate, everyone moving their tassels from one side to the other. There had been a moment when she was up on the platform, alone, looking out at the world, when she thought she might become something.

But later, when all the parents and dates, live-ins, and spouses had come to congratulate the graduates, Paul wasn't there. He had a perfect reason not to be, she found out when she went to his apartment: He was throwing up. He had gotten drunk with his boss, a very embarrassing and difficult scene for him. He would make it up to her, to both of them, of course. Remembering this, she realized she had eaten half a can of fudge sauce. She wouldn't be hungry for the dinner he was buying at a special place with especially good French white bread where he had gone to lunch.

She called and told him to change the reservations. She told him she was dieting. They could go anywhere he wanted since she wouldn't be eating. She knew he would be pleased, and he was.

After the call she watched a movie from the fifties. The wife was pale and delicate and screaming at the dark shadow of her husband.

*Cynthia and Konrad should be back soon*, Eleanor thought. They had a nice dinner waiting for them. She thought about the nice dinner Paul would be having too. It was a good thing she had gotten a check from her parents so she could pay for it. He had gone through his money drinking with his boss. He would pay her back, of course.

She thought about the beans fermenting in her stomach along with the fudge sauce. She thought how uncomfortable it was not to be able to sit up straight, to have to stretch out like a plank from the floor to the back of the couch because of her swollen stomach. She thought she could hear the timer and smell the beans burning. She thought Cynthia and Konrad had better come back soon because she wanted to go for a walk. She thought about breaking Cynthia's TV. That was what she was thinking when she threw the can of fudge sauce and watched it collapse on impact with the yellow living room wall.

Huge slugs of chocolate were crawling toward the carpet when Cynthia and Konrad returned. Eleanor was still watching TV though she had stopped stirring the beans.

"At the crucial point!" Konrad screamed.

"I'm going out for a while," Eleanor told them after she abused them for the dirty hairbrush on the kitchen table, the dirty dishes covering the kitchen counter, and her missing chocolate Dream Puffs.

By the time she had her tennis shoes on, she was done yelling and out the door. Cynthia never stood a chance, Eleanor felt, and she liked it that way.

She thought she was just going for a walk somewhat far away, but she kept noticing "Apartment For Rent" signs. She took it as an omen that she was supposed to inquire about the rent to help Paul decide whether to buy a complex. Single and studio apartments went for fairly reasonable rents, not a good investment probably, she would tell him.

As she looked, she was glad she wasn't moving. It was so difficult to decide. Then she found a little rental house. Somebody could clean the carpet and linoleum and tear up the dirt to make a garden in the back. It had white walls everywhere; it was wonderful; it was empty; it was nothing like Cynthia's apartment or her parents' house. She took the phone number. Perhaps Paul could make a deal and sublet it at a profit, she told herself, hiding the number in her wallet. She hurried home. She was late. But luckily Paul had called to cancel.

The next day Cynthia liked watching as Eleanor put Cynthia's name in the blank marked "Pay To The Order Of." Eleanor signed the rent check and said, "I think I might be moving soon." That was when the fight began. When the fight ended, Cynthia had decided Eleanor would be moving right away. Cynthia was keeping her check and finding a new roommate. Cynthia was punishing her.

*Eleanor is tired of being punished,* she thought as she moved her things out of Cynthia's apartment. *Eleanor is tired*, she thought as she locked her new door behind her. She was glad Paul had left a message saying he had been called out of town. That way she didn't have to tell him why she couldn't eat dinner with him or where she was living. She was glad she wouldn't ever have to graduate from anything again.

# PART THREE

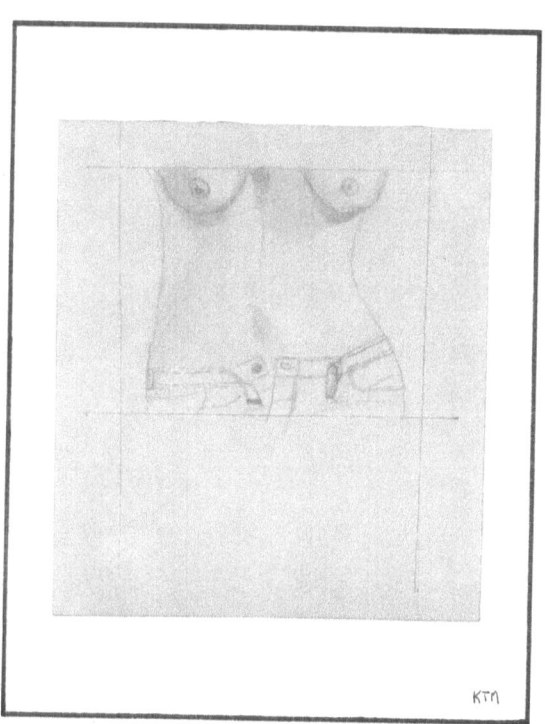

KTM

Eleanor sat on her living room floor reading a note from her friend Mark who had graduated and moved back home to Pittsburgh to live forever. She had asked him what he did for a good time.

"The thing you have to do is date," Mark wrote. "That's what I do. I date. I play softball and date. You either have to play softball or go paddling in a canoe, and you have to date."

She was sorry he had gone away.

*Everything you know is wrong,* she told herself, but she couldn't get very far with the idea. It stretched out and turned white at the ends like some hairy fallen creature.

When someone from college invited her to a party, she thought she would go for a good time though later she thought she had made a mistake thinking they were there for a good time. Still, intermittently, a good time was had: placing hands in men's hip pockets, stroking the cords of their jeans, mingling tongues, laughing at difficult jokes.

"It's fun to have a secret no one knows and to laugh about it when the time comes," someone said.

"I have a secret," Eleanor said. "In about a week I will be laughing at it."

She laughed, but she could not tell the secret, so no one else laughed. At the party it was fun when they each understood what the other was talking about.

People at the party enjoyed watching the police helicopter

beam its lights on another party. That was the kind of party it was, where people were vicariously at other parties. At least she thought that was the kind of party she saw as she watched other slices and mounds of the party strewn about the backyard in clusters like trash after the wind blows. She assumed certain things by the way the pieces of the party made only small molecular movements. She assumed boredom. She equated activity with not-boredom. At a party music could stand for activity, but there was no music.

As she talked, she shredded Styrofoam cups and drew men in around her as activities. Her blue stretch top and right hip became points of interest at the party, at least for some. She realized that for others the party was quite a different thing. They were working on getting jobs or exchanging methods of teaching English or math.

She talked to a new boy who said his name was Jeremy and he was a painter; then, he went to tell some other people some other things. She talked to some other boys while she waited for him to come back. Sometimes she kissed them while their girlfriends weren't looking, and sometimes they kissed her while their girlfriends were looking.

A man she didn't know introduced himself. He listed all his credentials then tried to stand under her arm where another boy was standing, but the boy wouldn't let him, and the man went away.

Eleanor saw him watching her and realized he was forming his image of the party by making a story about her, a story with many male characters and long hands. He would think the slice was the whole story; it would be narrow and twisted, she could see. It would have to pass through his pockmarked face and thinning graying hair before it could revolve in his brain, gather pieces to itself along the wall of its centrifuge, before it could be peeled off the inside of his mind like so much pressed paper. She didn't want to read that story, see that paper. Motivation, so important to the story, could only be fragmented and cliché, could only seem insightful and complete.

But like streamers of newsprint stuck in her hair, his story followed her outside the party to the front walk and goodbye. His story opened with the repugnancy of the smell of patchouli, an old cliché smell from the sixties, he said. A bad beginning, she who wore patchouli should have realized right away, but she was busy leaving, heading toward activity, going dancing, swimming. Jeremy, the painter, was waiting.

The man making the story was willing to give her a chance, he said, though what the chance might be for she didn't want to imagine. She left her thoughts unpictured, thinking only in white light. She allowed her thoughts to disperse, to squirm off in threads of color.

He asked about the boys, the pockets, the tongues, and how she perceived them. She did not perceive them, she told him, she did not perceive well at parties.

He, though, was an amasser of perceptions, a root ball of perceptions. He perceived her as frantic, useless, groping, not of his needs, he told her as she explained about the party, the dancing, the boy waiting, the quest for a good time.


One Saturday Eleanor decided to visit the store she had discovered, Nicole's Closet, where the clothes came from all the dressing-up dreams of frizzy-haired blonde Nicole. She wanted to visit Nicole's mother too, who sold Mary Kay cosmetics and encouragement in the back room. Mrs. Stevens was a heftier image of her daughter with the same raving blonde hair, a friendly horse's grin, and huge breasts.

Eleanor wasn't sure how to greet them after seeing their picture advertising the Christian Women's Aglow. In the past she had said, "Hi! What the hell you all doin'?" She didn't know how to talk to Christians, but she liked them. They acted like they had a secret and loved everybody and were happy.

She went inside to hug everybody and say hello, but when she noticed Mrs. Stevens, Nicole, and Nicole's friend and employee, Stephanie, enraptured with opening a gift, she put her hands behind her back respectfully and was quiet.

Beneath Stephanie's thick precision-curled bangs, she looked about sixteen of her eighteen years. She lifted a small rectangular present wrapped in bright pink paper out of a brown sack and handed it to Mrs. Stevens. It was Mrs. Stevens' birthday, Eleanor realized, and felt embarrassed. She had come uninvited and without a gift. Slowly Mrs. Stevens unwound the package like she was removing a bandage from the skinned knee of heaven. Eleanor was jealous.

Inside the paper was the word "Jesus" made of preserved bread dough. Its soft fat folds were painted brown.

"It looks like a string of hot dogs!" Nicole said and laughed.

But Mrs. Stevens held the sacred name balanced in her hands and read it aloud: "Jesus." She slid it onto the counter like a careful priest delivering the host and hugged Stephanie.

With tears in her eyes Mrs. Stevens said, "Thank you. That's wonderful. And you made it."

Stephanie nodded and smiled.

Mrs. Stevens rewrapped the gift and put it in the sack; then, she and Nicole gathered their matching hot pink plastic totes.

They had an appointment with the owner of another store, they explained. As they got their hot pink spiked heels from behind the counter and put them on, Eleanor wondered how it would be to look like her mother instead of like the opposite of her.

"Don't you want to see what a big girl looks like in a little pair of hot pink French-cut pants?" Eleanor asked, but they were waving and gone.

"Nicole and I are best friends," Stephanie said twice as they talked about who Nicole was dating.

As Eleanor carried a pair of lavender slacks and a pair of black ones from the sale rack to the dressing room, she asked, "Do you go out with anyone?"

"No. I date a lot of guys," Stephanie answered, swinging the half-door of the tiny dressing room open for Eleanor then letting it close behind her.

"Oh. I thought you were the type to get married," Eleanor said as she tried on the shiny black pants, hoping to get something in case she was asked out.

"No. Why? Where did you get that impression? I'm curious to know why you thought that." She was insistent.

Eleanor looked over the door to see Stephanie at the counter organizing big bead necklaces and bright ceramic pins. Eleanor wiggled her hips into the pants thinking, *Because you look like you're trying to catch someone.*

"I don't know," she said. "I guess I figure everyone wants to get married sometime, you know." She looked over the door again.

Stephanie was facing the mirror on the side wall, lifting her short flounced skirt to pull at the top of her pantyhose. Eleanor wondered what it would be like to have legs like that, going straight into her underwear instead of curving all around.

Stephanie answered, "Oh, I get lonely sometimes, like everyone, but that passes, like the feeling that you need someone." She adjusted her rear-length dark hair in the mirror then touched her eye shadow. She looked at Eleanor as she fluffed her skirt. "Anyway, the Lord's going to come and do away with this world. I can hardly wait. It's getting to be a powerful burden to bear."

Eleanor zipped her pants. "Oh, you're waiting for the Lord instead of a man?"

"Yes," Stephanie answered the mirror, looking into her own blue eyes and freshening her dark red lipstick. "It's getting to be a powerful burden to bear."

Eleanor didn't know what to believe. She was thinking too many things.

In bed it was exciting for Eleanor to read the little book Mrs. Stevens had given her, *Delivered from the Devil*, by Harley Wilson, the evangelist Mrs. Stevens had promised to introduce her to. In his photograph Brother Harley was so good-looking, so obviously charismatic, that certain distilled portions of his life gave her little rushes as she read about his searches for "female companionship": "Every night I found a woman I could satisfy myself with, not caring if I ever saw her again."

Eleanor wondered how many women he had now that he had a board of directors and a schedule of Rescue Missions and Teen Challenges. A rodeo roper for Jesus, he stood pictured in boot-cut Levi slims and a leather vest, a Bible for branding in his hand, and the wind in his thin curly hair, a witness for weathered health: "Put your hand in the hand of this man." He had been a country-western star, a Grand Ole Opry hit: "All I had left of my riches and reputation was a Fiat Spider and forty dollars," he wrote. She turned to "GENERAL GUIDANCE": "According to your FAITH be it unto you." Yes, that was general. She had no idea what it meant.

On Sunday Eleanor went to Brother Harley's revival with her new friend, Petunia, who worked as a clown at the mall where she met him.

Outside of a small stucco church in a neighborhood of sagging wooden houses landscaped with wheel-less cars and toys, Brother Harley interviewed the choir, a flock of teenagers driven in from the southern California beaches, according to the label on their bus. They were inspirationally handsome. They reported their names and transgressions to Brother Harley.

"I smoked marijuana cigarettes every Friday night after the football game," one young man confessed, "until I was saved."

A young woman reached for the microphone and said, "Through the love of Jesus I have found the reason for my being and for the being of all things."

Eleanor was impressed. Brother Harley was destined to save her, too. Mrs. Stevens had promised.

"Jesus is a person we can all have a personal relationship with," another young woman said.

Petunia nudged her. "If you want profundity, you know where you can get it," he whispered.

The choir broke up and spread into the crowd.

"Brother Harley saved us," they said, passing out handshakes and hugs.

Eleanor reached for them.

"I hope that'll motivate your ornaments," Petunia remarked.

She nodded vigorously.

Eleanor watched Brother Harley and a curly-haired brown-eyed young woman singing, delivering the microphone back and forth with small silent prayers. They sang of their love, their love of Jesus, asking the crowd and the chorus to join them like a great all-of-America-wants-to-get-to-heaven sing-along.

Petunia whispered, "I bet all he does is take her to porno movies. I bet he doesn't know any better."

Eleanor decided to postpone her salvation and come back later.


That evening she observed carpet, pews, a pulpit, and a cave inside the church. The back of the church where the congregation faced through three to five services a week was not like the First Baptist Church at home with its flying glass windows, but a hollowed-out rocky space, a cave.

*Do they take off their high heels and commune with the maternal side of God?* she wondered.

She was late. She had missed Brother Harley's sermon. She hadn't wanted to be told she was a sinner. She already knew she was a failure. *All we want is for you to be happy,* her mother always said. *And you're never happy. Why can't you be happy? I don't think you're ever going to be happy.*

A woman with rabbity pink cheeks, stiff gray curls, and a ruffled lavender blouse cushioned Eleanor's hand in hers as Eleanor entered the greeting line.

"No, I'm sorry, I didn't get to hear Brother Harley speak,"

Eleanor replied while reviewing her small knowledge of Christian symbolism: *Was the stable that Christ was born in part of a cave?*

More greeting hands, like friendly pistons, projected her down the line. Or—Christ was buried in a cave: *We pray to God, the giver of eternal life. The God who emptied the grave.*

They drifted outside where the chorus of beautiful smiling young people was holding hands. It was quiet where Eleanor stood beyond the circle of lights. She saw Mrs. Stevens in the distance, praise God, listening to the singing, hallelujah, watching the dancing, praise the Lord. The chorus was clapping and chanting, hallelujah, like they do it on the TV, praise Jesus. Confessing, brothers and sisters, leads to righteousness, glory, glory, these suntans and feathered permanents, hallelujah. I love you Jesus, and big crowds, and no drugs, but new clothes from mother. Praise God is love, is excitement, is screaming and shouting hallelujah!

Eleanor was depressed.

"Brother Harley can speak to you now," someone said.

Brother Harley scooped up her elbow and directed her to a low concrete wall. They sat, she scuffing at the dirt, removed from the fizzing afterburn of the crowd.

Looking down, she dumbly did battle with her fingernails until she heard herself say, "This is really hard. I want to ask some questions. I don't know what I'm doing, where I fit in, what I'm supposed to do with my life."

Frustrated and bored with her own nervousness, she forced her hands onto her thighs and watched Brother Harley flip through his Bible. She remembered what Petunia had told her: "Don't let them quote from their Bibles. Take their Bibles away. See if they can talk without quoting."

"The Lord has given you his only begotten son," Brother

Harley said. He closed the book emphatically and looked into her eyes. "The Lord has given you his only son. His son, Jesus, he has given you."

She asked him what he meant. She couldn't see how it applied. As he talked, her mind played among the bright colors stretching out inside the gray bursting shell between them. She noticed his beautiful eyes and hair and his smile that would crack a football mouthpiece. That was the kind of smile he had, one that reached back to his college football days.

Then he said, "Let the Lord help you with a drug problem."

"But I don't have a drug problem."

"Well, give this to a friend who does." He handed her another copy of *Delivered from the Devil.*

"But none of my friends have drug problems," she said, waiting for him to tell her to find some who did.

"You don't know much about me, do you?" he asked, excited. "Let me go get one of my books. Just wait here."

She watched him light up cluster after cluster of followers, looking for his life in a neatly witnessed tract. She imagined waving goodbye to anyone watching and saying, "Yes, we've finished talking. I have to go now." Then he turned away from the crowd, toward her, and she made herself stay.

He sat on the wall again.

"I just feel confused about my life, about everything, about what I'm supposed to do." Her words reverberated with unimportance. She looked up at the end of their glide to see that Brother Harley's eyes were not on her but moving through his pamphlet, skimming the pages. He was not listening.

Her silence caused him to look up, turn toward her, and say, "The Lord God is your father." Pointing to the text he had written, he said, "Look, look here. 'The Lord God is your Father.' Isn't that amazing?"

She waited for more words and was startled when Brother Harley placed his hands in a grip on her head. Before she could ask more questions, she heard him say, "Oh, Lord Jesus, deliver this child from the devil of intellectualism."

"The devil of intellectualism?" She had not heard of that particular form of evil.

"Just try saying, 'Jesus, if you're real, come into my heart.'"

She repeated the words slowly.

As she finished, he proclaimed, "She's been saved!"

He grabbed her hand, and as she fought discreetly to pull it away, he led her to the crowd full of phrases and praise.

"She's been saved!" they shouted.

"She's accepted the Lord!" someone said then asked, "What's her name?"

Eleanor was impressed by their enthusiasm until she heard Mrs. Stevens say her name.

"Eleanor's been saved," the crowd repeated.

The curly-haired brown-eyed young woman locked hands with her, saying eagerly and from experience, "You've accepted the Lord in your heart as your Savior?"

The crowd clamored for reassurance while Eleanor tested the possibilities.

Ordering herself to want them to hear, she said, "No. No, I wouldn't say that exactly." She looked across their feathery heads to Brother Harley and felt the young woman's comforting hand drop away.

"She's been saved?" the jumping crowd asked. "She's accepted the Lord?"

Then their welcoming ended. No longer looking at her, but drifting around her like bumper cars slowing down, they patted and thumped and moved on.

As summer heated up, Eleanor got a daycare job and enrolled in life drawing at night. She went early to the first class to show the teacher her drawings so he would let her in. His name was Peter House. Some students who had been there before called him "P. House." It helped to think of him that way—pee house. Otherwise she couldn't concentrate to draw. Otherwise she kept looking at the line of contrast between his curly gray-blond angel hair and his fine tan forehead. There were too many other girls in the class who could draw better, she told herself. He would never ask her out.

He introduced the model, Kitty. They were doing ten-second gesture drawings. Kitty took off her robe and stepped onto the platform. Naked, Kitty helped him push huge wooden boxes into spaces and shapes. He dimmed the lights then raised the spotlights, which struck hard shadows across the wood. She was going to tell a story, she said. The light crossed her hips and face, reached for her large breasts, and let shadows fall there.

Eleanor searched for the single line of movement within each pose. The line kept moving, the search seemed random then became rhythmic as Peter called out the time for the changes. Kitty's face changed too, but it was all part of the gesture. The light on her body began to look blue. There was green and brown in the shadows then black, but Kitty's white shape contained the line of movement. Eleanor had to draw the white line, she knew.

The students paused, then started again while Peter watched

Kitty. She was in the woods, looking for something. There were men on horses after her, but she was naked and quick. She knew where to find the dark spaces beside the boxes. She stood hard to one side with her muscles clinched and was invisible. There was nothing to capture but a straight line.

Peter clapped for her story. "That was beautiful."

They began a longer drawing. Kitty lay on the platform on her side, her breasts against her chest like balls of white socks. Eleanor tried hard to draw them well, but the picture she drew was of a skinny old woman instead.

"Is that what you see?" P. House said, looking over Eleanor's shoulder.

"No, I don't think the angle here is quite right," she lied.

The next drawing was for a long time, too long. As Eleanor looked at Kitty, there began to be dark shadows on her face. She seemed two-dimensional. The shadows hardened into black and white and were no longer rounded. Her body became a geometry problem. It became part of the problem of the background and foreground. Eleanor tried to draw the white line of motion but could not find it. She stopped to sort out the white spaces and the dark spaces, the shadows, and Kitty. She thought at the break she would buy some brownies and offer them to her.

At the break, Gabriel—big, dark, hairy, expressive and attentive—introduced himself to Eleanor as they walked to the snack bar. They bought coffee and brownies, then sat outside on a concrete bench and watched a storm coming. The wind was blowing, and there was distant lightning. It reminded Gabriel of living on the beach in Mexico. There were storms all the time.

"For nights and nights I would be alone," he said, "but one night I met a girl. She was French. We couldn't speak, but it didn't matter. We drove to a high bluff overlooking the city, and we made love. She was beautiful, and I liked her better because we couldn't talk. It was wonderful to make love. It had been so long. But she had these long fingernails, and she kept crying and moaning and scratching me. It was ecstasy, one of the best times ever, but she kept moaning and scratching. My back was bleeding. I was glad I never saw her again."

Gabriel lit a clove cigarette and blew smoke out slowly. He tapped the ashes to the ground. "So you tell me a story now."

Eleanor drew in the ashes with her foot. "When I was little and my oldest brother, Jamie, was in high school, he used to practice with his band in the garage of our house. My older brother, Teddy, could go inside, but I had to stay outside. One night I was sitting by the door, and they came out for a break. One of the guys put his cigarette out on my head. He thought I was an ashtray, he said."

Gabriel laughed, and she drew in the ashes.

When they went inside, they looked at the drawings. Gabriel asked someone if he could have one. He wanted to keep Kitty forever, too. His drawings made Kitty look young and plump. When he put them beside Eleanor's, they made her drawings look tortured. He kept his things next to hers anyway.

Eleanor wanted to put the brownies she had bought for Kitty on the table, but Gabriel made her take them to her.

"Here," Eleanor said.

"Thank you," Kitty said.

"That was terrific," Gabriel said. "Your movements were wonderful. What was the story you were telling?"

"It was from a play I'm in. That's where I got the idea to tell stories, from acting. It's all acting. It's all stories."

When they started again, Eleanor saw a number line, thick

and black, that went across the paper then stopped. She put marks on it for Jamie's drum major's baton, his saxophone, and the mirror he had over his dresser, the one Teddy was left with. There were signs on the mirror, signs Jamie had left for their mother, signs their mother couldn't see, or had seen once then had become numb to seeing, or couldn't stop seeing, the way Eleanor couldn't stop hearing her mother scream at Jamie. "My day isn't complete until someone has given me hell for something," one of Jamie's signs said.

During the weekdays her mother screamed at Jamie because he had so much to do, because he was always gone, because he needed his dinner before his band practiced. On the weekends she screamed at Teddy. Jamie wasn't around then, so her mother couldn't scream at him, only at dinner on the weekdays.

After Jamie died, Eleanor asked if he had ever done anything right, if he always had a bad attitude, a chip on his shoulder, like their mother said.

"Jamie? Jamie was wonderful," her mother had answered. "He always did so much. He was always so busy. He always did so well."

"Why did you yell at him so much then?"

"Did I? Did I use to yell at him?"

"Yes, and Teddy, too. Teddy every Saturday."

Eleanor turned to a clean sheet of paper. She could go no further with Jamie and the number line for now. She drew Kitty again, focusing on her from the waist to the knees. There wasn't much time, but she drew what she could very carefully. When she finished she leaned back, deciding how to frame it. She got out her ruler. It wasn't difficult. The whole drawing fit inside a two-by-three-inch box.

After class, Eleanor watched Gabriel smoke a clove cigarette under the eaves of the building while it rained.

He wanted to take Eleanor for a ride on his motorcycle, "But it's no fun when it rains," he said.

"I had fun once when it rained," she said. "Want me to tell you?"

He said okay.

"When I was in college before, I visited my friend Rachel in San Francisco. She lived over a Chinese restaurant. We were bored, and she said she'd give me a dollar if I'd go lie out in the rain. She said it would make her happy, so I did. I lay down in the gutter. The water was about six inches deep. When I put my head back, my face was underwater. I would raise it and see people looking at me. It made Rachel laugh. That's pretty funny, huh, lying down in the gutter?"

"That's terrible."

That made her feel sad, but she leaned against his solid round body. He blew softly scented smoke into the air and put his arm around her.

"I like you. I'll be your friend," he said.

For a long time she just thought about those words, repeating them to herself. She put her arms around his thick waist, held on to his shirt with one hand, and felt the broad firmness of his back. She put her face in the dark hair in the "V" of his shirt and smelled cloves. She felt his thigh muscles huge and substantial against her legs, saw the palm trees waving in the rain and the night, and thought of nothing. His mouth was cool and soft when he kissed her. Their mouths changed shape inside together, the curving surfaces became round and hard then soft together, became warm together. Then he had to go.

"Don't worry," he said. "I'll be there for you. I'll be your friend."

"Don't say that. You can't know that."

"You can trust me. I'll be there."


"Tyro, the Greek sea nymph, one of three thousand daughters of a Titan sea god and goddess, had been immortal but died along with the culture which created her," Eleanor read in an art history book. That was sad, she thought, sadder than a mortal death perhaps. Mortals expect to die. They spend their lives preparing for it. Tyro though—elusive, playing in the heaven underwater—was caught surprised. Her tales were of sea pranks and innocence, the fears and flirtations of the pristine. What could have prepared her for her end, even if she died slowly over the centuries, during the fall of the Greeks, the rise of the Romans, their fall to decadence, then Christianity?

Eleanor pictured Tyro's curving sea-dancing body left dry by the water receding from the square farmlands of the Middle Ages. Where do the immortals go when they die? The mortal, they are made of energy, and that goes on. It is nothing for them to die, especially in the abstract. Death is only final for those who remember. But the immortal, they are made of less. Their death is permanent.

Twice each day when the tide rose, Tyro rushed towards the shore to meet her beloved Enipeus, a patient river god transformed by the jealous Poseidon into a restless blue-gray horse. As they touched, waves engulfed them, and she was drawn back by the currents to the floor of the sea, overwhelmed with ceaseless longing.

Eleanor wanted to reach out to Tyro, to call her back. Perhaps someday she would tell her students the legend of Tyro. Perhaps they, in their foreign culture, would cling and remember. Perhaps they would imagine her, give her a fishtail body swimming out of their arms. Perhaps Tyro's frail immortal life could be sustained a few moments longer.

One night crossing campus after class Gabriel asked Eleanor, "Are your parents rich?"

"They are now, but they didn't used to be," Eleanor said and started telling him the story of garbage soup.

Then Gabriel saw his old friend Joe, his best friend, he said.

"Hi!" he said to Joe.

Joe said, "Hi!" and walked on.

Joe was his friend from when they were five years old, from when they were in high school and took the train from Portland down to Mexico, he explained.

She went on with the story of garbage soup. "I think we were poor when I was little, but I'm not sure. My parents don't talk about it much."

"Wait a minute. You made me think of something." He headed to a payphone to call a friend.

"Hello, Dr. Anonymous," he said. He asked Dr. Anonymous to tell him a story. Dr. Anonymous told him the story. Gabriel handed her the phone so Dr. Anonymous could tell her the story.

"You have to say, 'That's life,'" Gabriel said.

She took the phone. Dr. Anonymous said, "This is from an old joke. It goes like this. You say, 'That's life.'"

"That's life," she said, and Dr. Anonymous said, "What's life? A magazine. How much does it cost? Fifteen cents. Only got a dime. That's life. What's life? A magazine. How much does it cost?"

While she listened to the story, Gabriel wrote it down. When the phone call was finished, Gabriel had to go to the library, and she had to go home because she had nothing else to do, but she still hadn't told her story.

"We used to have garbage soup," she said as she followed him. "My father would bring home old vegetables and meat scraps from the grocery store and make them into lunch."

"That's disgusting," Gabriel said then waved goodbye.


The next week as they walked to the snack bar on their break, Eleanor told Gabriel, "When we were kids, my brother Teddy did the neatest thing. Do you want to hear?"

"No," he said; then, he said "Yes" and laughed.

"Well, he was just a kid, maybe twelve or fourteen, and my father was punching him around the kitchen for my mom. Teddy was bigger than my mother, so my father had to punch him for her. My father was bigger than either of them. He hit Teddy in the nose, and it started to bleed, a stream of blood. Teddy didn't hit back or anything, he just walked into the living room, bent his head over, and dripped blood on my mother's new gold carpet."

She looked at Gabriel and smiled. "I think that's the coolest thing I've ever seen a kid do."

She was happy telling him the story and didn't care if he thought it was cool or not. It made her realize how much she missed her silent brother Teddy.

One evening Eleanor stayed after daycare taping the children's bright animal pictures on the milky green walls. *It used to be fun*, she thought, *sailing*. They used to sail to the tropics, the islands. Once when they got to the Arctic, all the animals were there. There was so much black and white, blue and green it was almost colorful though not like the jungle they went to. They used to visit all the animals.

"What kind of day is it?" the children asked them.

On a good day the fish answered, "Lightly slanting patterns. Mild vertical drifting."

Every night in her cottage by the wharf she sat at her kitchen window with its red geraniums and red gingham curtains. The people went away, and all the sea animals came—pelicans, seagulls, sandpipers, seals, and sea lions. Sometimes fish came, fish from far out at sea, the colorful tropical fish. They came to the edge of the water or sat quietly on the rails of the wharf. It was cool and gray. The fish talked among themselves.

"It's trying to be winter," they said. "It wants to be winter, but it's not time yet, so we are here instead."

The fish stayed calm against the drifting curves.

But now the animals are unidentifiable. They are a mishmash. They have no shells. The red crabs and the other animals surround her, but they have no shells. Only white meat remains.

She had wanted to live on the houseboat moored in the bay. She could see its silver windows shining, but it was drifting away. The wood had gone gray, the gray was lost on the gray sea, in the clouds and the night. Outside her window was the houseboat, but she was inside and it was far away.

She stopped staring at the pictures. There was no time to finish putting them up today. The pictures could wait. The story could wait. She could go home. She turned off the light that shined on the pictures and the green walls; then, they looked black.

*I have a melodramatic mind,* Eleanor thought as she stood at her kitchen table watching her new neighbor, Christiana, walking away. Over six feet tall, her shoulder-length hair pale blonde, her body drifting and thin like a piece of handmade lace, Christiana would never have to insist she was not like other people.

When Christiana's kitten, Huck, jumped on the table, Eleanor played "Bayonet Training," poking him with a pencil eraser until he jumped down. When he came back, she played "Funeral," putting a kitchen towel over him, pretending she had buried him. Then she played "Second Coming," lifting off the towel and raising him high to worship him.

Now that summer was nearly over, she hadn't gotten a teaching job, life drawing was over, and she hardly saw Gabriel, she was thinking about seeing a therapist. When she was in college before, she had seen several.

One said, "The only reality is your feelings."

"How could that be?" she had asked. Feelings were the only things that weren't real and could easily be changed.

"Your feelings are the only real things you have," the therapist had insisted, and Eleanor knew she was lost.

Perhaps another therapist would believe, as she did, that her savings account with $8,000 in it was the only real thing she had, but unfortunately her mother's name was on it, so Eleanor couldn't get to it.

"What seems to be the problem?" another therapist had asked.

"I don't know," she had said. She told him about her family though she was afraid it wouldn't interest him. She talked into her hands a long time then looked up. She needn't have worried about boring him. He was asleep in his recliner. She could hear her mother telling her, "Well, nobody likes to listen to someone complain."

Then Petunia called. He wanted to know if she wanted to go play with the adults. She said yes. They were going shopping, he said.

He arrived wearing a giant green and purple plaid tie and his long brown hair flowing. She gave him one of her embroidered pocket hankies to match his tie. It went well with his yellow suit, too. She put on her yellow plastic fog glasses and red galoshes then got her white Lloyd's of London paper bag her mother had given her as a present from her trip to England. It was double strength and had cord handles. Eleanor liked it a lot.

They rode the bus to the shopping mall. Inside, they took turns carrying the sack while they walked around backwards, smiling, as Eleanor had seen a bag lady downtown do, until it was time to go home.

At home there was a letter from her mother. Her parents had been to a Republican fundraiser in the nearby big city. Two of the football players who had lived in their house, Clint and his brother, Chad, were there. Eleanor was surprised. She thought she had made the football players up. Her mother said Chad was a sheriff and Clint was a secret service agent, but maybe her mother made *that* up.

"I almost didn't recognize them, it's been so long," the message said. "You remember Clint and Chad, don't you?"

She remembered, but it was strange her mother remembered too. They had so little in common. Eleanor wanted to see them and ask where they had been and why they had not come to visit. Maybe it would tell her something about Jamie, where his life might have taken him, and if he would have wanted to see her again.

"You kids had so much fun with those guys. I'm so glad they lived with us," her mother wrote.

Eleanor walked into the kitchen, went to the corner, and slid down the wall. She stared at the cupboards and bit her hand. She knew her mother wanted her family more than anything, and she couldn't have them; and Eleanor would do anything to be her mother's little girl again, to waltz with her in the kitchen after they had finished the dishes before her father came in. She knew somewhere they loved each other without language or manners or measures of success. And she knew that in this world her mother's anger was enough to kill her brother, to cause him to misjudge a curve or the speed of a turn, and she knew her mother knew that, and that there was no end to the horror of her sorrow.

As she cried, she said out loud, "I didn't mean to get this far away from home," and pounded the back of her head against the wall until she couldn't tell why she was crying anymore.


It was comforting to find she could walk down the sidewalk leaving a trail of snot and tears no one would see. *Was that a sign?* Eleanor wondered. *Was that sometimes a sign, when you walked down the sidewalk carrying groceries, crying?* At daycare the other workers would think it was a sign. They were trained to see signs there.

As she got closer to her house, she listened for Gabriel's motorcycle. That would be a sign. Often she would run outside, thinking she had heard it, and there would be no one there. He had promised to visit. Perhaps today he would come. Perhaps he would come before she cooked dinner. Perhaps they would go out to dinner. He liked to go out. Then she remembered it was Friday, and he played his guitar on Friday and Saturday nights. It might be fun to go clap for him and listen to him sing. It was the weekend, and she was supposed to have fun.

Thinking she might see him reassured her, but her hands were still limp and uncoordinated as she struggled to unlock her door. After she put the groceries away, she drifted into the bathroom. She would clean the sink. It was gray and stained. She wanted to see something, a sign, in the patterns of the stains as she tried to make them white. Gabriel often wore white. He was always in music, but he never danced. That was how Jamie had been.

Then she thought of roller skating. It would be cool and familiar inside the smooth white concrete skating rink. She could think about Gabriel, imagine him skating beside her, then tell him she had been skating and had thought of him. He would praise her independence. She would move in and out of the rhythm of the track with the fast boys, and when she went fast enough, concentrating on holding onto the ground with the edges of her skates, everything would be controlled by the music and round.

She woke up scared when she heard a knock at the door until she heard Gabriel saying, "Eleanor, wake up. It's all right. It's me. Answer the door."

"I didn't think you'd be asleep this soon," he said when she opened the door. It was after 2 a.m. He had his guitar in his hand. "I just finished playing. I missed you. I thought maybe you would come. You said you might. I thought maybe you were awake, so I decided to come." He hugged her, and she was glad.

"Do you have any coffee?" he said.

She offered him instant. He was going to leave, but she said she had made nut bread and asked him to stay. He sat at the kitchen table and played music while she made the coffee, set out buttered slices of warm nut bread, then watched the butter run off the bread, cool, then harden again. The coffee stopped steaming and oil formed on top. She stared at the muscles in his huge forearm. She thought about touching his hand, lifting it from his guitar, but reached out and touched his thigh instead. He played the song about the drunken sailor and his favorite one about the long cool lady. Eleanor acted happy.

She tried to talk to him. "What are you doing tomorrow? Do you want to do something with me?"

He said yes. He said he would call her, and they would do something. Finally he stood up and apologized for playing so long, for coming so late.

She thanked him. "It was wonderful. It doesn't matter. I can sleep in."

She walked with him into the living room. They stopped, and she put her arms around him and leaned back. His bulky strength made her happy. He admired her body and that made her happy. They kissed and moved against each other. She pictured them as two curved geometric forms filled with sand, one that could be poured into the other. She tried to fill her curved space, to take the sand she needed from him without letting him know she was taking it, without leaving anything missing, but the sand seemed to flow the other way: She could feel herself disappearing instead of filling up.

"I have to go now," he said.

"Can't you stay? I want you to stay."

"I want to stay, but I can't. Maybe someday I can."

"Why can't you stay?"

"I have obligations. Believe me, I want to, more than anything, but I can't." He opened the door and was gone.

In bed she hugged her pillow to her body thinking of all the times she had fallen asleep that way and all the boys who had gone away.

When she finally slept, she dreamt she was running through a forest of giant wooden boxes, the boxes Kitty had run through, only now they were bigger and were colored green, brown, blue, and white. They had no shadows. A white light shone evenly on them all. They were heavy and set at odd angles. Their sharp corners were jagging into each other. A young man was running behind her. She tried to make it be Gabriel, but it was one of the football players, her favorite, Danny; then, she wasn't afraid even though they were running. They were running for fun though the corners of the boxes made running difficult, and she hit them.

She could see her mother at a distance waiting for them to reach her. Children tumbled out from underneath the band of her mother's apron, rolling out as babies, hitting the bare wooden floor of the forest of boxes as two- or three-year-olds, then running off to play as smiling chubby five- or six-year-olds. Eleanor and Danny were excited. They couldn't stand still. Her mother wanted them to stop being silly. When they got quiet they could ask politely for what they needed. Danny wanted to know something, then Eleanor wanted to know it too, but her mother wouldn't answer.

They repeated the question, but her mother refused to tell.

Eleanor woke up forming the question, thinking *What is my name?* and for a moment could not remember then could not get it straight.

She spent the day in and out of bed, watching the windows, adjusting the volume of the radio, listening for Gabriel. When she heard too many motorcycles go by, she turned up the volume and drowned their sound out. Late in the afternoon he came. He wanted to take her shopping. There wasn't time to come in.

They went to a thrift store. After looking at Army jackets, Gabriel went to the slips and peignoirs. She helped him find the most interesting ones.

"Look at this one! Look at this!" she said.

She looked at the peach silk bed jacket he held up. He asked if she liked it, and she said yes. He had her try it on. It was a little small, but he thought it was sexy. She was surprised when he bought it and put the sack inside his blue work shirt.

Then he took her home. She hugged him and kissed him goodbye while he was on the motorcycle. He was late for work.

She watched him as he rode away, holding on to herself, seeing his taillight flash red over and over as he wove down the street. *I am not ten years old*, she told herself. *I can get control of my life. I don't have to always be so alone.*

# PART FOUR

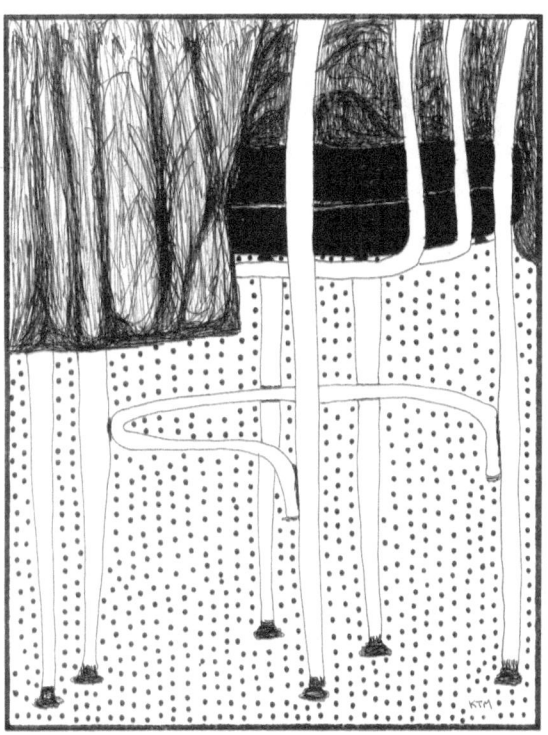

When her mother called asking when she was coming to visit, Eleanor hesitated in her reply, knowing her family would refuse to see her and hack hunks of flesh from her side. She could see the knife going into her ribs, cutting through so the entire chunk of her right side was removed. In reality, she could not say how they did this. Perhaps this time they would stop slicing at each other, but then there might be nothing left to do. That was what scared her most: They would put their knives down and not care.

"Of course you're coming home," her mother said on the phone. "You must be bored there, not doing anything. There's plenty to do if you come home."

"I guess you're right." Maybe she would go. Maybe it would be nice to see everyone. She would like to see Teddy and ride her bike.

After she hung up, she went to her refrigerator. It was empty. She supposed she could go home. There was nothing to keep her.

She walked outside to her garden. She couldn't go home. She had to water. She would have to call and cancel. Her mother would understand. She had houseplants.

Eleanor went in and sat by her phone. Why not go? There was nothing to do here. Sure, there were her friends at the pool, the ones she said, "Hi" to when she swam every day. But she'd get to tell them, "You won't be seeing me next week. I'm going home!" They'd smile over that one. "Going home, huh?" they'd say. She could ask her neighbor, Christiana, to water. It would give them something to talk about.

$A$s Eleanor flew over the hot western deserts she was glad she was not driving. She had thought about driving. She could have afforded driving, and her parents wouldn't have had to pay. She could go where she wanted when she got home if she drove, but her mother had insisted on her flying, so she did. Her mother liked flying.

Her mother picked her up at LAX. As usual, her mother was in a hurry.

"Where are your bags, dear?" she asked.

"Hello, Mother. I think we have to wait for them."

"I'll get the car and be in front. I forgot to tell you, I'm having a party tonight. If we don't hurry, the people will be there before we get ready. You're not tired, are you?" she shouted as she trotted out of the airport.

It was a two-hour drive home.

"It'll give us a chance to catch up," her mother said in the car. "We hardly ever talk anymore. You tell me everything you've been doing."

Before Eleanor could answer, her mother started talking about Tom. "I guess you haven't met him. He'll be there tonight though. He's such a nice young man. He helps me with the table and says such nice things. We met him hiking the Grand Canyon last year. Your father gave him a job for the summer. They went fishing together last weekend. Tom seemed to have a good time. He seems to like our friends. He's been coming to our parties, even though he's younger, just twenty-two. Everyone certainly enjoys having a young man around."

"Is Teddy going to be at the party? Did you invite Teddy?"

"I invited him, but he probably won't come. He has his life, and we have ours. That's the way it should be, don't you think?"

She agreed.

"Ray from the construction crew is coming though, and Rosemary is bringing her daughter. They should get along. I think they're about the same age, both in their thirties."

"So there'll be a girl for Ray and a guy for me," Eleanor said.

"No," her mother answered. "You're too old for Tom."

Eleanor thought she was going to get sick.


While Eleanor made stuffed celery and ranch dip for the relish tray, her mother tried on a pair of slacks and a long-sleeve top. Eleanor said she looked fine, but her mother said she was too hot. She changed into a skirt and summer top and asked if it was too casual. Eleanor shrugged.

Her mother wanted Eleanor to try the top, so Eleanor stood in her bra in her mother's bedroom while her mother took the top off; then, her mother stood in her bra while Eleanor tried the top on. Eleanor didn't like any part of it, including the top.

Eleanor was making a green salad when her father came home.

He said to her, "How you been?"

"Fine," she answered.

He sat down in his big recliner in the den and surrounded himself with the newspaper. That ended their conversation, but Eleanor had enjoyed talking with him.

Then her mother pirouetted from the bedroom to the TV in her new aqua dress.

"Do you like it? Does it look right? What do you think?" she asked.

"It's fine," they said, but it wasn't enough.

"What about the color? What about the ruffles? What about the cut?"

"Fine, fine, fine." But it wasn't enough.

Before her mother got enough, Eleanor had had enough. She went into the bathroom and locked the door, but her mother found her and made her come out.

In the back yard at the party everyone noticed Eleanor's tan. She thanked them.

Her father was tending bar and offered to make her a drink.

She said, "No thank you," and he laughed at her. She didn't usually drink. He thought that was ridiculous. She went back inside.

Every few minutes her mother came in to check her dress in the mirror and say, "It doesn't look like Tom is coming." Then she played with Eleanor's hair and asked, "Would you like to get it cut like mine?"

When Eleanor went outside to eat dinner everyone noticed her tan again. She had many thank-yous to say, but it was easier than talking.

During dinner the women planned what they would have at their next party.

"I'm bringing the salad, right?" Joan said.

"Dessert's mine," Rosemary said.

"You make the best desserts," the women said with an eager hateful cry.

"Thank you," Rosemary said.

Eleanor was glad she wouldn't be going to that party.

After dinner some of the men offered to help Eleanor in the kitchen. She put on her favorite apron, a watermelon print that came to her knees. After they brought in the dirty dishes, she sent them away. She didn't like them touching her.

Tom never came. But Teddy came to borrow a water ski. Eleanor saw him leave the yard door to the garage with it.

"There's Teddy!" the company said.

"Teddy? Teddy? Where?" their mother said. "Teddy, come here. Come say hello to the nice people." She laughed and extended her hand toward him, presenting him. He had on cut-off jeans, worn-out boxer shorts showing underneath, and a dirty T-shirt.

"Hello," he said reluctantly.

They all "Ooohhed" and said hello back. Teddy was good-looking.

"Hello," Eleanor said. She hadn't seen Teddy since Christmas when she was too sick for him to talk to her.

"Hello," he answered; then, he waved everyone off with his hand.

Eleanor went inside and watched him leave the yard. She wanted to grab her heart with both hands and twist it in her grip. If she could twist it tight enough, no blood could get to it, and her hands would stay occupied. What she really wanted to do was to run to Teddy, hug him, then if he tried to get away she wanted to pound him with her fists, but that was what her mother did to Jamie and he died.


The next morning Eleanor got up early to ride her ten-speed. She looked in the backyard and the garage, but she couldn't find it.

"Does Teddy have my bike?" she asked her mother.

"No, Tom borrowed it. Didn't I tell you?"

"No. Could I get it back?"

"We'll call him tonight when he gets home from work and see if he's still using it," she promised.

Eleanor spent the day reading and lying around the pool. Occasionally she swam laps, but the pool was so short the turns made her dizzy. When her father came home, he walked toward her then noticed her bikini and walked away. She felt bad that she made him uncomfortable.

That night she and her mother played cards. Her father sat in the den with them watching TV until she and her mother started talking and got emotional. He left the room to watch another TV. He didn't like it when they got emotional.

Her mother finally called Tom about the bike. He would bring it over the next evening, he said. Her mother said okay even though Eleanor had wanted to ride it the next day.

The next day was the same. Eleanor flopped around the pool and around the house trying to find something to do.

"Is anyone coming over this weekend?" she asked her mother. "Did you invite anyone?"

"Well, some people might come over, but we hadn't planned anything. We aren't expecting anyone. Why, are you bored already?"

"No," she lied. "I was just wondering."

That night Tom called. Eleanor's bike had gotten run over in his driveway that day. He would get it fixed soon.


Late Saturday afternoon Eleanor walked to Teddy's house to borrow his bike. He was in the garage waxing his Porsche.

"Why don't you go to Mother and Dad's parties? Don't you have a good time?" she asked.

"Why bother? The food's lousy—always hamburgers or some damn potluck thing. I can do better if I stay home, and the company's better even if I'm alone with the dog."

She laughed.

"I don't know where they find those big deal hotshot friends of theirs: Billy Williams, bank president, and all he can talk about is the last time he fell off his horse."

She laughed again. Teddy would only talk to her if her mother wasn't around. Growing up, the guys in her house would only talk to her if her mother wasn't around.

"You'd better get going if you're going to ride," he said. "The bike's over there."

She told him thanks and left though she wanted to ask him some more things, but it made her happy he had thought to tell her she had better go.

Her usual routes led out then snapped back like boomerangs. It was six miles south on the oil field back road to the small town where her parents grew up then back on the main road. It was six miles north through winding foothills to Valley Vista park returning on another main road. Another stretch east up a big hill then through a series of back roads went to no destination at all, but that route, with its long-abandoned inclines, was her favorite. She always looked for her father in his work truck. One time he passed and waved, but later he said he couldn't understand why she wanted to be out riding alone.

Because it was late she headed west to the small airport and circled around the edge of town. The sun was dropping when she passed the cemetery. She wished Jamie was buried there, but he was buried at the nearby city's big cemetery. She remembered as a kid riding past here in her mother's station wagon while her own best friend, Rachel, was talking about her older sister who died when she fell on the school playground and hit her head on the sidewalk edge. Rachel was four years old when she held her sister in the back seat as their mother drove to the hospital. Her sister died in the waiting room as her brain swelled. No one thought it was an emergency.

"If either of my brothers died," Eleanor had said then paused to think of them, "but especially if my brother Jamie died, I would never get over it."

Two years later Jamie was killed, and she had never gotten over it.

The day of Jamie's funeral, she had asked her mother if she could go to school. Her mother said no. Eleanor had gone to school every day since the accident and thought if she went to school everything would be normal. Her father had gone to his business as he had done every day. He came home and drove them to the funeral then went back to his business. Later she read stories about families who hung black wreaths on their businesses and closed them the day of a funeral out of grief and respect. She wished her father had done that. She wished her father would have cried, but he didn't, not for Jamie or himself or anyone. What he did was work.

On Christmas days Eleanor used to listen to the letters Rachel's father wrote in memory of Rachel's sister and read aloud to their family. Eleanor was envious that they were allowed to remember. She didn't want Jamie to feel he didn't matter, that he wasn't worth their parents' attention.

"Poor little Jamie boy," her grandmother used to say. "It still just about breaks my heart to think they killed him."

Eleanor imagined her grandmother only meant some vague force of evil by the word "they." Her grandmother would not have thought her parents guilty of anything.

"He was such a good boy, always doing something, working and all," her grandmother would repeat, but while Eleanor was in Arizona she died. Eleanor had not gone home for her funeral because no one told her.

Eleanor rode past her old high school. The college football players were practicing on the lighted field. She wished Danny and the other athletically charming young men who lived with them could see her now, now that she was not so much younger than they were, no longer chubby and immature.

The last two miles she pumped hard all the way up the hill. She pushed the gate open, slammed it shut, and staggered into the yard, her leg muscles tight.

Her mother was at the barbecue table looking at some photographs.

"Oh, Eleanor, come see these pictures. I just got them from Rosemary. They're from our trip to Canada."

Eleanor walked stiffly over. She welcomed seeing the green and the mist after riding through the dry fields.

"Here are some pictures of Tom we took." Tom was muscular, tan, cheerful like the football players had been. Tom alone in front of the surf. Tom with her father in a boat. Tom with her mother on a porch. Tom with both her parents, their arms around him.

"Tom sure is good-looking," Eleanor said.

"Oh, isn't he though," her mother answered.

The next night while Eleanor read in her room, her mother opened the door and said, "Tom's here. Come out and meet Tom."

In the den Tom was drinking beer and watching baseball with her father. They yelled and moved to the edges of their seats then yelled and sat back. Eleanor could see why her father liked Tom. He was someone to watch baseball with.

"Tom, this is our daughter," her mother said.

Tom turned. Eleanor was surprised he wasn't as cute as his pictures. He looked like he was stupid—something about his too-short too-blond mustache, the slow thick sag of his eyes and lips. Suddenly she knew her mother must be getting old. Eleanor wanted to laugh at Tom then remembered she was staring at him and said hello.

"Hello," Tom said and turned back to the baseball game.

If only he knew about the boys who had come before him who were so much better-looking, so much brighter, he wouldn't be so confident about his blond hair and tan, she thought.

Her mother sat down on the couch next to Tom. "I'll be in here if you need anything, dear," she said.


*The keepers of our culture are the ladies of the afternoon,* Eleanor thought as she helped her mother lay out the silver and china on the card tables covered with white tablecloths. Her mother had been baking and setting up all morning. No one else would care but the ladies who played bridge.

"Everything has to be perfect, doesn't it, Mother?" Eleanor said.

"Well, it's the bridge group, dear. When I go to the other ladies' houses, I feel so ashamed. They do everything so wonderfully."

"It's going to be fine, Mother." The flowers looked nice, even if they weren't in matching vases.

Eleanor went to the kitchen to check the butter cookies in the oven. They were turning brown around the edges.

"Don't burn those!"

"I didn't burn them."

"Well, dear, it's for the ladies."

Eleanor took the cookies out. She arranged them on plates and carried them into the living room.

"Don't put those cookies out yet! We wait until later, when everyone has come, before we bring things out."

Eleanor put the plates on the kitchen counter. She was tired of helping.

She went to her room and fell asleep on her bed. She woke up when she heard the doorbell chime and the ladies coming in. She had heard those sounds all her life. They made her angry still. It meant people were here, and they would take her mother away.

She listened as her mother apologized for the sherbet: "I couldn't get that good kind, the Ruben's. I'm sorry. They were out of it."

"That's all right," one woman said. "I'll have some next time. I'll order it early to make sure I get some."

"Oh, Helene, what happened to your linen here?" another woman asked.

"What? What is it?"

"There's a spot on it. It looks like coffee. Have you tried soaking it in baking soda?"

"No, I haven't heard of that. I'll try it. I'm sorry."

Why had her mother wasted her life on these ladies, Eleanor

wondered. She loved her mother so much more than they did. They didn't even help her carry things or try to make her feel better. Eleanor wanted to grab her mother's hand and take her away. She wanted to bring back all the bouquets of flowers and homemade cards she had given her and pile them up for her. She wanted to set up tea for her dolls and invite her mother, and this time her mother would come.

"Eleanor, come and meet everyone," she heard her mother call.

She got up. She didn't mind meeting the ladies, they were so warm and polite and clean. In the living room she shook their hands and rubbed her strong tan cheeks against their soft powdery ones.

"Eleanor, would you get the cream and sugar? You forgot to put them out," her mother said. "Rosemary wanted some sugar, and there wasn't any."

"Yes, Mother. I'm sorry."

She got them from the kitchen and put them on the tables. This time it was harder to smile, and she wanted to get away.


That afternoon at the town pool Eleanor recognized a woman who had been Jamie's friend sitting on the deck with her two children.

Eleanor introduced herself. "I'm Jamie Lihte's sister."

"I wondered," the woman answered. "You look so much like him."

"I know."

"I still cry every time I hear someone play the horn," the woman said. "He loved it so much. He worked so hard. I still think about him, and I've been married for ten years. He was a really special guy."

Eleanor nodded. She decided to wait until she got home to cry.

The woman asked her to tell her parents hello. "They are so nice."

Eleanor nodded again and tried not to feel crazy.


When she walked into the house, her mother was sitting at a card table with her shoes off.

"Hello," her mother said. She sounded tired. "Did you have a nice afternoon?"

"Yes. How was the bridge group?"

"Well, I didn't win any money. The ladies were glad to see you."

"That's nice."

"Did you want something?" her mother asked.

"No, I just wanted to be with you."

"Well, I guess you should help me with these dishes." Her mother got up and carried things into the kitchen.

Eleanor made piles of dishes at the tables. It was impossible to talk.

Later, standing at the sink with her mother rinsing the dishes and loading the dishwasher, Eleanor said, "Those ladies weren't very nice to you."

"What?"

"Those ladies. Your ice cream was fine. Who cares if it wasn't Ruben's? And how come they can't help you bring in the dishes afterward? You didn't seem very comfortable around them."

"Those ladies are my friends. We have certain ways we do

things. I was the hostess. I'm supposed to take care of things. Those ladies are all very nice to me. I don't know what you're talking about. Are you the expert on making friends now?"

"No. I'm sorry. I know they're very nice. You just didn't seem very comfortable. I don't know."

"I've known those ladies for over thirty years, ever since your father decided we would live here. Now, what's wrong with that?"

"Nothing. That's great. I'm glad you have a lot of friends."

"I don't have a lot of friends. We just see the same people. But this is where we live. Your father's business is here, and this town has been good to us. I've known those women since you were kids. We had our kids together. It was hard as hell when we had all three of you."

"I know. It must have been." Eleanor knew how unhappy they had made their mother, demanding her attention, needing to be entertained. She still couldn't keep herself entertained.

"My life has not been terrible," her mother said. "We had three wonderful kids, and your father has done well. We have a good life. We always have."

"I know. You've been lucky."

"All except for your brother Jamie. Not every family has to go through something like that."

Eleanor heard herself asking, "What happened to Jamie? The babysitter said he had a broken leg. In the hospital I never got to see him. I can't remember the last time I saw him."

"You wouldn't have wanted to see him," her mother said harshly. Her eyes were red, but Eleanor knew she wasn't going to cry. Her jaw was set hard. "For a month I watched him in that hospital bed. I watched him curl up, turn black, and die. You wouldn't have wanted to see that."

Eleanor looked at her mother's angry face.

"You will never get over him, will you?" her mother said.

"No," Eleanor replied defiantly then went to her room and cried for Jamie, and for what her mother must have seen, and for not having known.


That night Eleanor sat in the den with her parents watching TV. The phone rang. Her mother went to answer it. Eleanor could tell something was wrong. It was the same voice she used when the hospital called about Jamie. It was something about Teddy.

"What?" she asked when her mother came back.

"Let me tell your father."

"Yeah, what is it?" her father said, sitting up in his chair.

"It's Teddy. That was the hospital. One of the instruments slipped at work. They're afraid it cut the ligament to his thumb. They're taking him into surgery now. He had them call us. They'll call us back in the morning to tell us how it went."

"In the morning?" Eleanor said. "You have to go down there now. He might need you." She thought of when she had walked home from the hospital alone. She didn't want Teddy to feel like that.

"There's nothing we can do," her mother said. "He's in surgery. They'll call us in the morning."

"You have to be with him! You have to go!" She was afraid her parents would let something happen to Teddy.

"Eleanor, it's late," her father said. "There's nothing we can do. They'll call us in the morning." He was disgusted.

She had tried to be so good, but now she couldn't stop screaming. "No! You go down there! You take care of him!" She knew she couldn't make them. She walked to the doorway then screamed again, "You have to go!"

"We're not going, Eleanor," her father said. "Now calm down."

"Then I'm going. Don't leave him alone!"

"It's awfully quiet at the hospital this time of night," he said, laughing at her. "Are you sure you want to sit there for nothing?"

She looked at her father as he sat in his recliner. She felt her face twist open, and she screamed—a loud wordless noise. She knew she must look horrible to him. She went to her room, slammed the door, and didn't come out until they called about Teddy in the morning. His hand was going to be all right.

Her father wouldn't speak to her, so her mother wouldn't either as they ate breakfast and drove to the hospital.

When they got there, Eleanor rushed into Teddy's room. "Teddy!" she said and started to hug him, but he pulled back, his bandaged hand raised in the air.

Her mother came in and hugged and kissed him. He mumbled hello to her. Her father was the only one who knew what to say. He and Teddy talked about how much work Teddy would miss and how it would affect the plans for the development they were surveying. Eleanor and her mother stood in opposite corners of the room and watched. Intermittently Teddy smiled at his hand.

Eleanor didn't know what to say until it was time to leave. Then she said goodbye and hugged Teddy. It would be a long time before she saw him again. Her parents were taking her to the airport that day, and she was flying away.

# PART FIVE

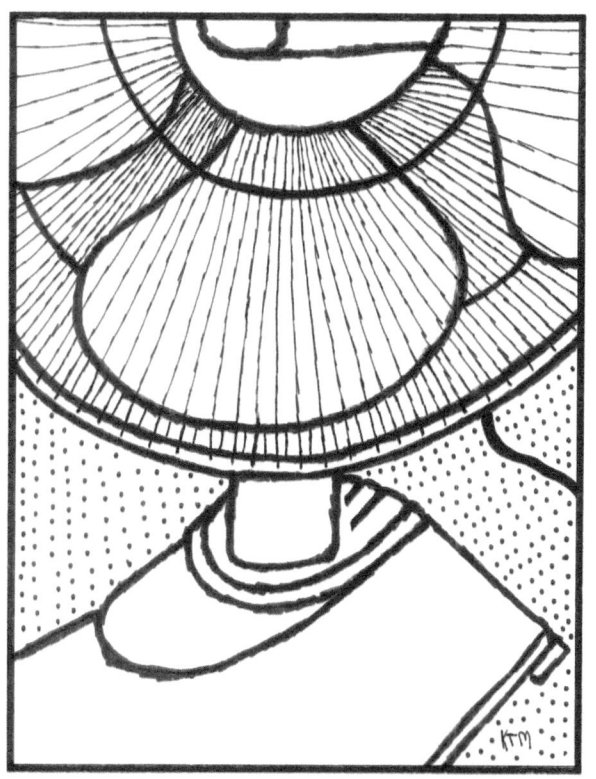

*"I'm a Ranger Bob, you're a Ranger Bob,*
*We are Ranger Bobs all, and when we get together,*
*We give our Ranger Bob call: "The trees are your friends!"*
*—a song from children's camp*

It was getting dark outside as Eleanor stood in her bedroom unpacking. She saw her father as he had looked at the Los Angeles airport, saluting goodbye to her from the distance of his high carpeted platform.

From her pathway she returned his salute: "Goodbye, stone father."

How does it feel to be the child of this hard sand-surfaced father? The feeling was pinned to the back of her like a large waving kite on a short string and followed her wherever she went as again tonight she made her way back from the stone father's house to her own.

"Stone father, I'm home," she said out loud.

The walls of her house were empty and white. There was nothing to fill them. They slammed into each other. Their many corners enclosed a loud noise and a space that was empty and white. She stood near one piling of corners, lost.

She couldn't have the stone father, she knew now. She had the corners and the walls. She was nowhere now, in dead space. The stone father had left only his indifferent salute to her. She started to giggle. She hid it with her hand.

She began singing "I'm a Ranger Bob" and hoped the stone father was not listening. This song was not for the children of the stone father. Their songs had been taken away. Their songs were in the trees now, away from the stone father and his children who remained. "I'm a Ranger Bob" was a song about another father, a different father, one with trees. The stone father never listened to trees, so the verses were safe.

She slid back across time to the stone father's house where he never listened at all, it seemed, until she was on the phone accidentally humming "I'm a Ranger Bob"; then, he would come on the other line. She would put the receiver down, ashamed. This father had built her first house, a stone house, keeping out dearth and dissolution with his knowledge of smooth hard stones. When she left she had wanted to take those stones and not just songs of trees. She wanted her smooth white corners to be built of stones. She wanted to hum this on the line for him, but there were no songs for stones.

"Where have you gone, stone father?" she asked the white wood corners of her house.

She invented gladness over soft things and tucked herself into bed, singing. Now she hoped not to find the stone father, but he was there. She had his image in the palm of her right hand. She lay in bed, spread eagle, crushing it.

In the morning she would turn the pages of the newspaper with her crushed hand and read about the death of the stone father, but she would not find peace. That only the stone father could give, and he was dead stone. If his death would make any difference she would be glad, but it wouldn't. Maybe if her hand healed it would make a difference, but it was too early to tell.

But the past goes on, and in it the stone father laughs. He is outside his house talking to the neighbors, and he laughs. She steps outside to be near him.

"Ha, ha, ha," he says, looking briefly at her.

But she is not the joke. She is only the child of the stone father. She goes back inside. She does not laugh. It has been so long since the stone father has made her laugh that neither of them plan for it anymore.

While fixing dinner, Eleanor went into the living room and kicked at her couch. She had begun beating the furniture at night. Sinking to the floor, she stared at the carpet thinking of the plastic brick house of her childhood. It crushed easily. There was green paper for a roof but no people. Her father came in at night and stepped on it. An accident. She built it again. Her mother had bridge. The house had to be moved. She dropped it. There were chips in the pieces. Mother said don't cry, put it together, again. It was only a garage without the broken pieces. The cat tried to sleep in it. It crashed. More broken pieces. She had to use them. The house was ugly. No one would live there. The holes looked like cockroaches. She kicked it. The government said she must rebuild. There were too many broken pieces and not enough people. There was no insurance. She could not rebuild. It was too sad.

She thought maybe Gabriel would come visit. She dreamed herself loved in his movie drama eyes. She would send him anything—a piece of toast; a leaf; a numb finger, red bulb at the end to detect heat; postcards every day—perhaps then he would come. She tallied his reactions like stones building into and tumbling down from a castle. She wished she were a dog—brown-spotted, floppy-tongued—chasing rabbits, mice, any gift to give him, knowing only dead things would suffice. She felt like plankton, falling through the blue waters of space, her arms outstretched like a star.

One night she went to a movie about a young woman who was going insane. Because the young woman didn't know what to do, she moved home with her mother. She stayed in her bedroom, the safest place.

One day her mother called out, "Some men are here to see you."

The young woman was happy someone had come to visit her, but the men only wanted to tie a white jacket around her and take her away, kicking and screaming.

Her mother said, "I'm sorry you never learned to get along. I hope you'll be happier now. Goodbye."

Eleanor left the movie crying so hard it was hard to find her car. Driving home she was still crying. The many lights along the street blurred long and fuzzy. It was hard to see where things were.

The next day she could not stop crying. She wanted to call Petunia, but when she thought about it she cried more. When she went swimming, the chlorine hurt her eyes and made her cry more. At the grocery store there were so many people she cried in the parking lot and couldn't leave her car.

Back home she wanted to call a therapist. In the phone book it was hard to find the right category then pick the right person then push the right buttons in the right order. When she finally got through, the receptionist put her on hold. She tried to hold on, but she couldn't. She smashed the phone down so hard she broke it.

She sat on the floor, holding the broken phone, and cried. She didn't want to buy another phone. She didn't want to shop or spend money. She was supposed to save her money. When Jamie died, he finally stopped costing money. Her parents were glad he had saved his money. They used it to pay his hospital bills. She was tired of calling out anyway.

"When something is too hard for me to do, I set it up so I do more and more of it. That way at least at first when there is so much more to do, it seems less hard. Last week there were some hard times, so this week I am going over them. Now last week seems much easier though this week has been very hard," Eleanor told Altea, the therapist, who took down notes.

"It began with a boy—twenty-six, dark, hairy, culturally good-looking—going through the motions of biting a glass. Can you see his twisted grin as it crunches?"

Altea nodded.

"He said, 'Most people look through the glass,' and held the bottom to his eye. Then he said, 'I want someday, someone to bite the glass. Rrrahh.' And pretended to crush it with his teeth.

"At first he said, 'I'd like to talk to you for about a hundred hours.' 'And then we'd be finished with each other and could move on to other things,' I said. So after talking about a hundred hours, but mostly in silences, we've moved on to other things."

Eleanor lifted her long hair from her neck with both arms, lifted against space that was collapsing on her from the walls.

*But love*, she had thought, dragging broken baggage, trash, rags, the chair into the waiting room. *But love*, she had thought as these were heaped upon her, handed to her, exchanged, replaced. *But love*, she had said to each note not left upon the door.

"Why do we believe certain people are more honest than we?" Altea asked.

*I've never talked to anyone like this before*, Eleanor's high school boyfriend had said, the college football players had said, the boy with dark curly arm hair had said. But Eleanor believed them all. She believed it was all true, that it had never been said before, that everything was new and unique and temporary and gone.

"All the boys have honest eyes. They all tell stories so well. They all leave notes. When I leave, even for a moment, I know I will return to a note one of them has left written on the backs of old poems, flyers, postcards, whatever they find in the mail."

"You said you felt shy, uncomfortable in the light," Altea said. "Afterward you turned on the light, pulled open the curtains, sat cross-legged on the bed, and waited until morning when it was light again."

Eleanor nodded. "I smelled like heaven. It was because I smelled like someone else. It was the heaven of having someone break through this world of blank papers and neat tabletops. I turned on the radio, for voice, and held the shirt he had touched, for smell, and had only thought left to myself, and the papers, and the tabletops."

Altea went on writing.

*Do not be impressed*, Eleanor thought. *We are dying in unimportant ways here: a case of light brown hair seized in payment for kicking, dreaming, for things like cloves, curly dark arm hair, glass.*


"We've kept no written documents," Eleanor told Altea at their next appointment. "We are travelers. Our stories move with us. They are not worth the trouble to carry. They fade, become untrue. I am a learner, born a princess, but now a learner in our tribe. There are no records, but there is a story I could tell."

Altea nodded.

"It has two colors, red and green. The jacket is red, and the walls are green. The red jacket gets torn in a room with white walls and gold carpet. A boy, over six feet tall, athletic, handsome, is wearing the red jacket. A girl is pulling on it. She is younger than he is, a few years younger. He is running, laughing. He turns. The jacket rips. He accidentally hits her. Her mouth bleeds a little. He is sorry. She is glad he is sorry. He will put his arm around her now. He asks if she is all right. She is all right—his arm is around her now. She holds her lip and looks at the tear in the jacket. She is sorry now, but his arm is around her, and she can keep the red jacket. She doesn't cry though she could, but then his arm would go away. If she doesn't cry and her lip doesn't bleed and she doesn't tell, nothing will happen, he won't go away, there will still be evenings and white rooms in which to play.

"Later there are other rooms, different boys, more torn jackets, torn T-shirts. Jeans will tear, usually at the seams, though sometimes at the knees. The hems tear, especially if the pant legs flare. If you are falling and the hem gets caught, it will tear. I learned to sew. I fixed the jacket. I never wore it or gave it away. None of my pants have tears.

"Now the room is green—an ugly milky green. The walls are concrete block. The carpet is dark green. The couches are old and heavy—brown and dark green. It is my old college dorm lobby. There is a TV on, but we are watching the walls instead, waiting for something to do. There is a party in another lobby. We have been there, but now we are in this lobby. I take off my green Army jacket. I am glad I am not wearing my red jacket. It would get torn. My red jacket is in the closet at home. This is not a long story. This is the middle already. I will tell you the beginning, then the end, then it will be over.

"I live off the study lobby. I have for a long time. We like our lobby though it is too quiet, and we are bored there. It is green there also.

"At the beginning of the story I am getting ready to go to the party. I put my Army jacket over my overalls. People on my lobby call me the Dutch Boy painter because they don't know my name, and I always wear overalls.

"When I walk out to go to the party, two boys are standing by the reception desk holding the phone. 'Do you know an Eleanor Lihte?' they ask.

"I take the phone. It is someone wanting me to come to the party. While I am talking, the boys talk about me. 'Who is she?' they say. 'I've never seen her before.' 'Look—look at her. Look at her hair. Look at the way she's dressed. Her hair's all cut off. It's practically shaved. She looks like a Marine.'

"When my call is finished, one of the boys says, 'Who are you? Do you live here? How come you did that to your hair?' I hit him in the stomach. He is tall and soft and awkward. He bends over at the waist. It is too easy. He's almost already falling. I grab his head and take it down with me. I am on the ground with him, but he is bigger, so I win. His buddy is watching. His buddy knows I win. The ceiling is green there. I stand up and walk away, brushing myself off. 'Watch out for Marines,' I say.

"At the party I tell the story, and everyone laughs. I point to the boys, and they also laugh. There are other boys there, the boys I watch the walls with later. We go into their friend's room and look at his books. We wrestle there. Their friend comes in. We leave, not wanting to wrestle while he is in his room. No one gets hurt.

"In the end, I am in another green room, my room, looking at the ceiling. I am in the top bunk. The light pushes on my head. I want to go to my art class, but I can't though it is time. My head hurts. I want to cry, but my head hurts. I am tired and scared instead. I will tell my art teacher why I couldn't come to class. He will understand. I have told him things before. I want to tell him because then I won't be scared. I can still see the couch, the floor, the wall behind the couch, the trash can, the boys, why they put me there, why my head hit the wall, why they didn't understand. I should have worn the red jacket, but it would have gotten torn. I could have shown them the tear in the red jacket, how I mended it, how it got there. They didn't understand. I didn't want them to go away. I wanted to be friends. I wanted to win. The walls were hard. The floor was hard. It hit my head. I woke up all day scared. I never told. It didn't end."

Altea nodded.


Eleanor began dreaming of her mother. Thinking of her mother took up unnatural portions of her time, sleeping and waking.

"In the dream I am home alone with my mother," Eleanor told Altea. "It is not our real home, it is more bohemian, but in the dream it is our home. My bed is an alcove between the den and the kitchen where my mother is most likely to go. There are no doors, so everyone walks through.

"In the dream my mother comes at me from the kitchen with a knife. She wants to have sex with me. She wants me to get on the bed, take off my clothes, and spread my legs. She holds the knife over my head so I will do this. I don't want her to touch me, ever, and she wants to have sex with me.

"Then she wants me to touch her. She lies on the bed with her legs spread open, naked, holding the knife over my head. She is an old woman, not old and gray and dried out, but preserved like some fruit, rotten under the skin but only slightly wrinkled on the outside and still covered with pink fuzz. She knows what she looks like and is horrified like I am. She pretends she doesn't, but she does.

"I twist the knife out of her hand and run down the hall. I want to get away, but she runs after me. At the front door she catches up with me and won't let me out.

"In real life this happened. One time I was home from my old college, we were in the kitchen, and she was screaming at me. I tried to get away, but she backed me into a corner and blocked my way. She held a knife aimed at my face. She wouldn't let me leave. I wanted to kill her. I wanted to pound her face and make her stop screaming, but I just tried to get the knife away. Then I pushed her and ran to the front door. She ran after me and tried to lock me in. I kept pushing her hand away from the lock, but she kept fighting back. Finally I just watched her lock the door; then, I unlocked it and ran away.

"In the dream it is the same. I only want to get away. I don't want to kill her. But she will not let me get away. She is not smart enough to pay attention, even when I have the knife in my hand. She won't stay away even when we are angry, my brothers and I. She laughs at us. She feels we are meaningless, insignificant, because we are only the children, and she is our mother.

"At last I get the door open, run across the street, and get into my car. My mother is behind me. I am scared, shaking. I lock the doors so she doesn't get me. I start the car. She scratches at the door then stands in front of the car, so I have to wait.

"Finally I can drive away, but then she is in an identical car beside me. I am on the right-hand side of the road, driving like I'm supposed to, but she is beside me, on my left, driving in the wrong lane. She is driving from the passenger's side, so she can scream at me.

"We head up the street to where it ends in a retaining wall. We are driving too fast. Two boys are crossing in front of us. I stop my car to avoid hitting the boy in front of me, but my mother keeps driving. The other boy has to run to avoid being hit. I see my father and our neighbor talking in the neighbor's yard, standing above the retaining wall. My mother smashes into it.

"I get out of my car and run toward them screaming, 'She's crazy! She's crazy!'

"My father screams back at me like he always does, 'She's not! She's not!'

"But for once I have evidence. I scream at him, 'Look! She's smashed the car! She almost hit a kid! And she's driving from the passenger's side!'

"He cannot deny this.

"'She's driving from the passenger's side?' he asks.

"That's all. He's seen it," Eleanor said. "He's seen that she is crazy. I want to believe it's true. I want to believe she's crazy. I want to show them it's not me."

Altea said, "You might never be able to show them. They won't ever want to see that. You just have to believe it's true. That dream may be all the proof you get. They may never defend you. They may never accept you. They can't afford to."

Eleanor wanted to know what she could do to make things better, to make her family like her.

Altea shook her head. "There's nothing you can do. When are you going to realize this is just going to keep happening?"

"But I don't ever know what's going to happen."

"When are you going to realize you're not going to get what you want from them?"

"But they're nice to everyone else. They just aren't nice to me."

"Because they don't have to be. They know you're still going to be there. You still need them. You have to change your expectations. They can't give you what you need."

"But they're so unhappy. I feel sorry for them."

"They don't want your sympathy. They want you to think everything is fine. They want you to respect them."

"I know I hurt them. I hate hurting them. Sometimes I'm mean to them. I want to be good to them."

"You aren't really hurting them. They're happy with the way things are. They get everything they want. You do everything they want you to. It's just hurting you. Stop thinking they will be there for you. They won't."

"But they're my family."

"Depend on them if you want. But it might be better if you made a life for yourself, stopped thinking about going back."

"I guess you're right," Eleanor said.

Driving home she thought about the bag ladies on the streets. Though no one loved them, they tried to live on. She wanted to know how they did it. She wanted to know what they were thinking as they got through each day. But most of them couldn't talk anymore or make any sense when they did.

One night Eleanor dreamed she was ten years old, waiting for Jamie's wedding to begin. Standing at the altar were Jamie's best friend and Jamie's girlfriend, the bride-to-be. Everyone waited, wondering where Jamie could be. Eventually Eleanor noticed his girlfriend's beautiful tiered wedding dress was not white but a dark blood red. Then she knew Jamie was not coming, he was dead, and everyone else would soon know. In her sleep she began crying, and she was still crying when she woke up.

"He was the only bright spot in your world," Altea explained. "That is why you miss him so much." She said a traumatic loss in childhood was the most difficult thing to recover from. It made it almost impossible to trust in life again.

When Eleanor had her teeth cleaned, the cute young dentist wanted to pour plastic into the tops of her molars and bicuspids so she would never have cavities. She agreed. His assistant propped her mouth open with instruments, and the dentist squirted the plastic in. It had the sweet vaporous smell of airplane glue. He told Eleanor to let him know if she was uncomfortable, but he didn't tell her how. When the plastic leaked out of one tooth and settled between her cheek and her jaw, the chemicals that would harden on her teeth and prevent them from rotting forever began melting her skin.

As she concentrated on the burning lake of skin, she wondered how deep and wide the fire would spread. Tasting the sweet plastic flames sliding down her throat, she wondered how toxic they were. She wondered if she should say something to the dentist standing hazily over her talking to his assistant. She wondered if she were able to say something, which she wasn't because of the instruments in her mouth, what she would say and what the dentist would do now that the plastic was where it should not be. There seemed to be no point in bothering him if she didn't know what she wanted.

She wondered if the fiery lake would cause her to start screaming involuntarily, making the dentist think she was strange. She wondered how long she could control her reaction to the pain. Already her hands, gripping the arms of the chair, shook, and her shoulders jerked. Her head was vibrating from holding it so hard. Her closed eyes were shooting red and white lights at her.

She was about to pass out when she heard the dentist say, "Eleanor. Eleanor. Are you okay?" She thought he was only being rhetorical. It took her a while to realize he wanted to know. The time was almost up for the plastic to harden, and the pain was subsiding, so she nodded and stopped twitching. When the instruments were removed and she could sit up again, she didn't think to tell him what had happened, and he didn't think to ask. She thanked him for making sure her teeth would always be perfect. He smiled and said she could give her check to the receptionist.

At home, when she saw the burned place in her mouth, she felt sick.


"You were going into shock," Altea said. "I think you've been in a state of shock your whole life."

She explained that everyone had a defense system, a way to protect themselves from the blows of the world, and Eleanor's was autism—numbing out, becoming mentally removed. Eleanor thought autism was when you beat yourself up and had to be restrained, but when she looked it up, the dictionary said "autism: absorption in self-centered subjective mental activity (as daydreams, fantasies, delusions, and hallucinations) especially when accompanied by marked withdrawal from reality." It seemed like a reasonable defense to her.

Eleanor's neighbor, Christiana, recommended that Eleanor go to a psychic to get in touch with Jamie.

After Eleanor told the psychic the story of Jamie's accident, the psychic asked what she wanted to know.

"I just want to know if he's okay," she said and started crying. She realized it sounded foolish, but she had worried that Jamie had been trapped in the accident and was still in pain, that he was not okay.

"Of course he's okay," the woman said. "He's fine. He's crossed over into the spirit world. He's been fine all along."

Eleanor nodded and kept crying.

The woman said Eleanor and Jamie had been together often in past lives. In Greek or Roman times they were the tall attractive children of upper-middle-class parents concerned with social appearances. As a young woman, Eleanor was sent to be a priestess in a temple. She was very lonely. Her parents didn't visit much. Her brother often came, but he was a soldier in the army and had to fight a war. He was killed in a battle. After that her parents came to see her even less, and she mourned for him the rest of her life. They had all agreed to come back to work out what was unfinished.

"Sometimes when we make these agreements from the spiritual plane, we think we can manage them, but they become much more difficult in the third dimension," the woman explained.

Eleanor nodded.

"Jamie was just trying to get away—he had to get out of the situation at home—you know."

She knew.

"He didn't mean to kill himself, but he went too far out of his body and couldn't get back. It was an accident. He is very very sorry. He wants you to know you have never done anything wrong. You are like twin flames—two aspects of the same thing. He is always with you, always protecting you. He thinks you are wonderful, and he is proud of all you have done. He loves you very very much. But he wants you to know you need to get on with your life. He is waiting for you. You will be together again."

Eleanor drove home crying, then got in bed crying, getting up only to drink water and go to the bathroom. When Petunia brought her a tiny green frog, he looked in the window and saw her curled up in bed with her hands in front of her face. He got mad.

Later Altea explained that pain and anger were the same, like when you curse when you stub your toe. She said it was better to show people anger than pain; they could deal with anger better. Seeing pain made people furious, not sympathetic.


When Eleanor told Christiana she was sleeping about eighteen hours a day, Christiana recommended a homeopath.

The homeopath looked up Eleanor's symptoms in a big book and gave her some tiny round white pills.

Eleanor asked what they were for.

"Madness with grief," the woman said.

Eleanor was glad there was a remedy for that. She took the

pills.

Driving home from the homeopath's house, Eleanor fell asleep. She pulled off the road and didn't wake up for two hours. When she got home, she got into bed and curled into the fetal position. She stayed there for days taking naps and eating toddler food—yogurt and soup.

When she called the homeopath for support, her husband answered. His wife was out of town. He said there was nothing dangerous about homeopathy. The remedy could be antidoted at anytime. She could stop the whole thing. But Eleanor didn't want to stop the whole thing, she wanted someone to help her. He said not to bother them again.

For weeks Eleanor lay in bed regrowing herself. Between naps, she wrote down every bad thing that had happened to her. She gave the pages to Altea and never saw them again. Her mother didn't like it when Eleanor had nothing to report in their weekly phone call, but Eleanor figured she would rather hear nothing than what was really going on. Altea thought she should be out getting on with her life and meeting men, but Eleanor didn't think so.

One night she dressed up and tried to walk downtown, but the cars kept coming at her with their headlights. They seemed to get sucked into the negative energy she was letting go of, and she was afraid she was going to get hit.

# PART SIX

When Eleanor finally got out of bed, she saw that her face had shifted. It was softer now, not as much like Jamie's, more like in her grade school pictures but not as fat and miserable. She began imitating the motions of a confident young woman secure in her place in the world. Instead of telling herself she didn't fit in, she found a group of other adult children and learned there were families more dysfunctional than hers. One woman was a twin, an unexpected duplicate, whose identical sister was the favorite in a family of five older boys while she was the scapegoat, raped repeatedly by her father and brothers from the time she was twelve until she married at seventeen. Recently as she worked as a counselor for war veterans, her own horror stories came back to haunt her. This was a typical pattern, which was what group was all about. A form of sanity was supposed to develop when you learned your problems were no worse than anyone's.

The *Reader's Digest* also helped Eleanor adjust to life the way it was. In it were people like Boy X who was afraid to eat spaghetti because he had seen his sister's brains smashed out, running red and white, by their stepfather wielding a frying pan while their mother watched. After years of institutions and therapy, someone finally asked him to tell what happened. He did, then climbed out from under the table where he had been hiding and went on with his life. Eleanor was inspired by these people. Her life had been so pleasant in comparison.

Altea recommended a book about "visioning," a new psychology trend: "Spend ten minutes a day recreating your past.

Imagine things better than they are, and they will come to be." Eleanor created new parents for herself, Mr. and Mrs. Mirror-Reverse. They looked the same as her parents but did everything the opposite. When she talked about her ideas, they answered back on the same topic instead of talking about food or personal appearance. When she was sad, they told her they were sorry instead of yelling at her. When someone was mean to her, they said she was right instead of the other person. This improved her mind very much until the phone rang, and she had to talk to her real parents. Altea didn't have much advice on how to handle that. Altea warned Eleanor she couldn't change everything but promised to help her adjust to life the way it was. Eleanor felt sorry for life the way it was. It seemed to be such a pathetic limping thing.

One day Eleanor realized she wasn't crazy anymore. When her mother was horrified that Eleanor had attended a movie by herself, she saw that the horror was attached more closely to her mother than herself, and that she, Eleanor, might not be horrible for going to a movie alone. She knew she saw the world differently from most people, but she didn't feel the urge to talk about it. She didn't feel the urge to talk about anything. She was learning to accept the human condition. Her previous resistance to it had made her self-centered and nuts. She told that to Altea in the message she left canceling her appointments.

At the grocery store, a kid out front selling newspapers was harassing people who didn't buy from him. He was about twelve years old, skinny, with butch hair. He had a bruise on his forehead and a cut on the bridge of his nose.

"Hey, batter. Hey, batter. Hey, hey," he said to Eleanor. He was wearing a baseball cap.

"Hey, how you doing?" she said.

"I'm fine. The kid's doing fine. Buy a paper," he said and grabbed her hand.

"Is there something interesting in it?" She pulled back her hand.

"Hey, buy a paper. Buy a paper from the kid," he said to an old lady walking by. She didn't buy one either.

"No breaks. No breaks. Never a deal for the kid." He shook his head.

"Okay, here's a quarter." Eleanor held it out to him with one hand and reached to pat him on the top of the head with the other.

"No hands! No hands! No hands on the kid!" he shouted.

"I'm sorry. You're right. No hands."

He took the quarter. "It's okay." He hunched his shoulders and pulled at the top of his T-shirt then took off his cap and straightened it. "It's okay. The kid's okay."

"I'll talk to you later. You take care," Eleanor said and walked into the store. She wondered if she had been as difficult to love. In her way, she probably had.

Eleanor began substituting at a high school whose motto was "Excellence by Design." First period, a tall awkward boy with tennis shoes about size thirteen opened the long plastic curtains in the science lab for her by stepping up on the counter and running around the microscopes and terrariums, dragging the curtains back because the cord was broken. Apparently no one had requested it be fixed.

During third period a boy came in late with his arm inside

his short-sleeve T-shirt pretending it had been amputated. A fawn hoof was attached to the end of his sleeve with a rubber band.

"Don't make fun of my stump," he said staggering around the class, waving the hoof about with his shoulder. "Don't make fun of my stump." He had a bright blue plastic ring clamped around his eyebrow.

He sat at a lab table and laid his head down. Eleanor asked why he wasn't working.

"I forgot my book at home," he said.

*This is excellence by design*, she thought.

One teacher allowed the students to give each other massages. At least this is what they told Eleanor when she told them to stop. It was too painful to watch them caressing each other, their bodies relaxing under each other's hands.

She spent much time telling the girls not to hit the boys. The boys were passive and conditioned to take abuse. Lining up at the lunch bell, the aide, a woman about sixty, hit them. They begged the aide to leave them alone.

When the boys hit the aide, she turned to Eleanor. "They're picking on me! They're picking on me!"

"You started it," she said.

Another day a girl couldn't get her computer to do what she wanted, so she pounded the mouse against the table. The kids grabbed at her, trying to stop her.

"No. Leave her alone. It's okay," Eleanor said, using her arms and hands to form a protective half-circle around the girl. No matter how expensive the equipment was she was trying to break, it was cheaper than a lawsuit, Eleanor figured.

Eleanor did not want to imagine the chaos that would ensue when these children reproduced, but obviously they were planning to. Boys and girls carried around dolls made of muslin and five-pound sacks of flour. They arranged with each other for babysitting. The dolls had to be changed, the students insisted when Eleanor told them to concentrate on their work. When they fed their dolls during class, she had to tell them to put their bottles away. They marked on a daily schedule all the activities they performed for their dolls' care. They got credit for this in homemaking, the only course they seemed devoted to. They were not allowed to bring their real children to class because it was too distracting, but they were allowed to do this.

Eleanor talked often to a mentally disturbed boy who otherwise talked to no one.

"What do you get if you take one child and add one year without discipline?" he asked while doing a math problem.

"What does it add up to?" she replied.

"Yes. What does it equal?"

"Well, a very young child without any discipline, without anyone watching over him, can get himself into a lot of trouble," she answered, thinking first of a toddler and then of Jamie. No one had been watching over him.

The kid nodded confidently. It was just as he suspected.


One day after school Eleanor sat at her kitchen table picturing a bright red balloon filled with happiness and adventure flying at the end of a white string in the pale blue sky. She wished she could give it to her mother, but as she imagined passing it to her, it turned into a hunk of raw beef; the string became a dangling vein. She did not want to give her mother a hunk of beef—she was too tied down to that—but already her mother was in the kitchen putting garlic into the meat for the party she thought Eleanor's father wanted. The thin squiggly vein was disconnected and useless. This often happened to Eleanor's gifts to her mother.

Eleanor imagined her mother standing at the door of her big red car wearing a white jumpsuit and smiling an untortured smile. She wasn't pretending to be happy or nice, she was happy. She looked like she was going to bridge, but she was too happy for that, Eleanor decided, and had her mother drive to the mountains. She was nice when she said goodbye, so she didn't have to call Eleanor "dear." She could call her by her right name.

That evening she had her mother stop at a little restaurant overlooking the mountains with silver and roses and white linen on the table. She ate a meal served by handsome waiters. She was alone but not lonely. She wasn't saying, "I embarrassed myself at golf again today. Rosemary plays so well. She plays every evening, but I have to stay home and fix dinner. My golfing just makes me sick, but I think it's more important I fix dinner, don't you, dear?" Eleanor wanted her mother to be happy because sometimes when Eleanor was taking care of her students, she saw herself as a huge sow stranded on her side with a mass of piglets sucking at her, and she felt sympathy for her mother.

Eleanor still told Gabriel "I love you" every day, but usually he wasn't there when she said it. Most of the time he was with his girlfriend, he had to admit. Eleanor worked on her love for him like the pillow she had embroidered when she was a child. She had had no idea what she was doing, but she pushed the needle in and out the way she seemed to want to, and the flowers and butterflies in her head came out somewhat scrunched and thick but colorful and pleasing to her nonetheless. Unfortunately, by the time the pillow was finished it was covered with dots of blood. It had lain, unstuffed, at the bottom of a drawer ever since. It still looked like nice work to Eleanor though.

Her love for Gabriel was the child she kept home from school. They sat on the couch and watched TV together. She would hold him, stroking his soft hair off his unfevered forehead. They liked the same blankets and the same shows and would get Pepsi and change channels for each other until late in the afternoon when it was time for her to cook dinner for her love.

She knew it was unhealthy, the way she treated her love. If the principal at her school knew, he would think her unfit. She knew her love should be directed toward some outward goal. She should encourage him to play football in the streets with the neighbors. She should be a crusader for her love, become involved with the PTA for him, but she was not one of those mothers, so she kept her love at home.

One night she let her love go out without her. He was a teenager now, more independent and difficult to control. He was going cruising with the boys he told her as he slammed the door. Eleanor, feeling young and reckless herself, decided to go out too. She took a long time getting ready, finding little things to do, but the time came if she were going to go, she had to go now. She shut the door and went to the bar where Gabriel was performing.

Gabriel's girlfriend was there. Eleanor was surprised to find herself being friendly to her, but it was easier to find room for that since her love had gone out and was no longer cuddled up next to her on the couch. In fact, Gabriel's girlfriend was pretty interesting to talk to, not because she was interesting, but because Eleanor thought it was interesting to talk to her.

When Gabriel came over, it was less interesting to talk to him. He was becoming pretty predictable, but this girlfriend was a new aspect to her love. Gabriel's girlfriend wanted Eleanor to come to their house. She wanted her to come over anytime. Gabriel wanted her to come over too, he said as he put his arm around his girlfriend.

Eleanor knew if her love had known about this girlfriend, he would have come along and not gone out with the boys. Her love would be infatuated with the girlfriend's thick pouting lips and the incredible thin length of her. He would have been pleased and amused by the fact she curled the ends of her soft blonde hair. Because Eleanor knew her love would have appreciated all of these things, she paid careful attention to them so she could tell her love about them.

When Gabriel touched her behind his girlfriend's back, Eleanor knew she should be moved. But all she felt was the obligation to be moved. If they had been at home on her couch, there would be so little room left because of the girlfriend, her love, and the blankets, Gabriel would barely fit. He would get shoved to the edge of the couch, up against its winging arm. When he tried to reach for Eleanor again, she was too far away to be touched at all. She remembered to smile and wave at him when she saw his hand. She remembered before it had pleased him when she smiled and waved at him. It had pleased him because he had a girlfriend and wanted nothing more, she knew now. She hoped it still pleased him though she really didn't care.

When the bar closed, Eleanor had several Polaroid photos of the evening to take home to her love. She knew he would be pleased. Gabriel's girlfriend was gone. Eleanor waved goodbye to Gabriel as he wound up the electric cord from his microphone.

She was happy to be going home. She had a lot to say to her love.

One Monday Eleanor realized she had missed her mother's Sunday call. She had unplugged her phone when she was cleaning. If she was bleeding somewhere in an accident, as her mother would think she was, she would be dead.

Because she didn't have time to call her mother before work, all day she thought she was dead though her normal life went on: The students still asked a lot of questions, the principal still smiled at her in the hall, and she still ate spaghetti in the teacher's lunchroom. She wanted to tell the other teachers she was dead, but they would only think she was strange.

After school she went to a workshop on controlling children. The speaker, the mother of seventeen kids, some adopted, some her own, warned it wasn't easy to change children's behavior. "When you don't react in the expected way, kids will speed up their bad behavior. If you give in, you have to start back at square one."

Eleanor thought of her parents peck, peck, pecking away at her like inquisitive woodpeckers because she was changing. Ever since she got her teaching certificate her mother had said, "Have you gotten a job yet? Do you think you're going to be able to get a job? Why haven't you gotten a job? What if you don't get a job? You know, you don't have a job." Now that she was working, her mother said, "Aren't you awfully busy trying to hold down a job? How are you going to look for another job? You still don't have a real job. Are you going to make more money at your next job?"

Recently Eleanor asked her mother if she was a mistake since she felt so unworthy and ill-conceived.

"I'll understand. Really, I will. These things happen all the time. It's perfectly natural. Most people are here by mistake."

She thought it was very mature of her to support her mother in the woman-to-woman way she was capable of now. But her mother said no, she was not a mistake, she was planned, which made Eleanor feel better about exactly nothing. If she had been a mistake, everything would have been much easier to understand.

Monday night as Eleanor lay on the couch waiting for her mother to call and say how worried she was, her guilt about being dead weighed her down like six feet of earth. Her guilt was so heavy she couldn't call her mother herself. Besides, after she apologized for making her mother think she was dead, her mother wouldn't want to hear about her real life. Her mother would rather be worried.

Eleanor felt so anxious she looked down at herself: dirty sweat socks, pink legs, black shorts, yellow T-shirt. If she was not dead, then what? And if her mother was not trying to call her, then what? And if she did not want to call her mother, then what? Then her mother did not really want to talk to her, knew she was not dead, and would assume she could make her feel guilty next Sunday when she called and said, "I tried to call you last week. Your phone rang and rang. Where were you? I was so worried about you." But Eleanor would know she hadn't tried that hard because the phone had only been unplugged a few hours, and there was nothing to worry about. She was not dead yet.


On Sunday Eleanor told her mother how busy she was. Her mother said, "You'd better be careful. You're burning the candle at both ends!" That was what she had shouted at Jamie. Eleanor told her father she was sending his gasoline credit card back then ended up thanking him for sending another. She felt like a totem pole, standing on square one, with two woodpeckers digging at her head.

She could feel them pecking at her as she put on her shoes to ride the bike she bought now that she was making money. "Get out of here! Leave me alone!" she screamed, her hand slapping at the air.

She went to the mirror to put on her sunglasses and helmet. "Goddamn you!" she screamed at herself, her fist raised. "Goddamn you stupid no good, you stupid. Stupid kid. What the hell do you think you're trying to do anyway? You stupid!" She put on her bike gloves as she was screaming.

She saw her father—the terrible swift hand of God—reaching down for Jamie as he tried to get away. "Get back in here!" she screamed for her father as he pulled Jamie through the windshield of his car as it smashed.

She saw her father running after Teddy, ready to smash him. "I'll knock your head off if you don't straighten out and do what I say!" she screamed like her father.

As she was screaming, she realized why she was so afraid of men like her father. They could smash your head right off if they didn't like how you behaved.

Before she left the house, Eleanor screamed at herself, "Get back in here! You're bothering people. Leave those people alone! You're disgusting. Get back in here! You little shithead. Get over here!" She thought it was funny her parents were so angry about her. It made her feel less angry about herself.

"Who do you think you are anyway?" she screamed as she put her feet in the toe guards and headed down the street. "What are you doing? Get back in here!"

On the road as she picked up speed, she felt free.


One Friday walking toward her bank with her paycheck, Eleanor saw her old boyfriend Paul walking out.

"Hello," she said. She thought it sounded crisp and polite, exactly appropriate after a year-long separation. She reached out to touch his shoulder, but it felt awkward. The bank was large and impressive, and no one else was touching in front of it.

"Hello," he said, making an equally brisk and appropriate acknowledgment.

"How's your Mustang?" she asked.

"I sold it. I made quite a lot. I bought a Z."

"Oh."

Paul looked at his shoes, then at a girl walking by wearing black high heels and a tight black miniskirt.

"I still have my car," Eleanor said. He hated her car. He thought it made her look pathetic. "I just had the clutch rebuilt."

He shook his head. "Do you have a job yet?"

"Yes," she said. Altea had told her she didn't have to explain everything to everyone, so she didn't say she was only substituting. Then she remembered he owed her forty dollars for the seat covers she bought for him when she did that sort of thing.

"Do you remember when I bought those seat covers for you?" she asked.

"What?"

"Those seat covers, for the Mustang, remember? I thought maybe you might have it with you, the forty dollars. You said you'd pay me back."

She was scared he had forgotten. She was scared he thought

she was lying. She was scared she wouldn't get her money back.

"Yeah, I remember."

"So, can I have it?"

"No."

"I want my forty dollars." She was really nervous now. She felt out of control. The forty dollars was in Paul's control, and she wanted it to be in her control. She thought of things forty dollars would buy.

"No. You can't have that money. I don't owe it to you."

"It was my money. You asked me to buy them for you."

She saw her father watching her get ripped off. He thought she was stupid: "I never made a friend or a buck by loaning money," he said.

"I want my money," she repeated.

"No. I'm not going to give it to you. You don't deserve it."

"It's mine! I want it!" she shouted.

"You don't have to make a scene."

She felt embarrassed and stopped making a scene though really Paul should be embarrassed. He was stealing her money.

"You were supposed to pay me back."

"Well, I'm not going to. I earned it." He put his hands in his pockets and looked at her then walked down the street and got into an orange Datsun Z.

She went into the bank and deposited her paycheck. She couldn't understand why she didn't deserve the money. She walked out of the bank toward her little yellow car thinking the forty dollars was hers.

She started crying as she was driving. Fortunately, she had had a lot of practice. While she was driving and crying, she imagined going home to her bedroom and crying. That made her cry more. She imagined grabbing the money from Paul's wallet then shopping for herself with the forty dollars. That made her cry more.

By the time she got home, she had stopped crying. She went to her bedroom because that was what she had planned, sat on her bed, and stared at her closet. She'd never done anything to Paul. She'd done everything for him. She imagined taking him to court; then, everyone would know she was right. He had been the one who was so insensitive.

Finally she realized maybe Paul was hurt when she left him. Maybe he had invested something of himself in her. Maybe he had liked her and didn't know what was going on. Maybe she didn't deserve the money. Maybe she'd been awful to him. Suddenly she felt okay that he had kept the money. Maybe there was justice after all. She smiled at her closet and got up to wash her dishes. It would be wonderful to have everything in order again.


The day after Eleanor got home from Gabriel's dinner party, she and Petunia decided to give a party of their own. It would be a cocktail party. It would be more fun than the dinner party, she hoped. That hadn't been much of a party with just Gabriel, his girlfriend, and her, but it was something they all felt they had to do.

Eleanor and Petunia's party was a response to that. They felt giving their party was something they probably shouldn't do, but Eleanor was tired of going to other people's parties and not having one of her own. At their party they were going to serve fried eggs. This was Petunia's idea, and Eleanor was only mildly against it.

At the grocery store they had fun choosing the eggs. Petunia chose big brown ones, and she chose little white ones. They were also going to serve tea. Petunia chose Pelican Punch, and she got Morning Thunder. At Gabriel's dinner party his girlfriend served pickled German roast beef with spiced cabbage. It gave Eleanor terrible gas.

Eleanor and Petunia didn't know who to invite to their party. They didn't have any friends in common. Eleanor wanted to invite Christiana, but she knew three was an awkward number. They decided to buy a newspaper and look for people who would be fun at their party. After all, they had already bought the tea and the eggs, so they felt they had earned the right to a good time.

It was fun buying the newspaper. They reached in and grabbed it before the trap door closed. Eleanor took the entertainment section, the recipe section, and the gardening section. Petunia took the sports, the front page, and all the other parts of the paper Eleanor wasn't aware of. She was getting to be smart about a lot of things, but she was still dumb about newspapers.

Gabriel and his girlfriend had been looking for a good time too when they invited Eleanor for dinner, but she had refused to give it to them. She had refused to help analyze their character flaws and left them feeling disappointed.

Eleanor and Petunia were determined not to be disappointed at their party, so they bought homemade green corn tamales. Already they were having a good time. The man who sold them the tamales smiled at them.

Eleanor wanted to keep their party simple. At Gabriel's party she had been expected to deal with a lot.

"I think we ought to deal with this," Gabriel's girlfriend said.

"There's nothing to deal with," Gabriel said.

"We could probably think of something," Eleanor said.

"You know, Eleanor," Gabriel's girlfriend said, "Gabriel latches on to girls like you all the time. He brings them over. He makes a big fuss over them; then, he drops them. I've seen him do it a million times. You're just another one of these girls, you'll see."

"You must get tired of that," Eleanor said.

Gabriel went to his room in the basement to get his guitar. His girlfriend went to wash dishes.

When Gabriel came back, he told Eleanor, "I don't know why she says these things. She wants it to seem like my friendships are meaningless, like she's the only person in my life. But that's just not so. She's so insecure sometimes. She has such a distorted view of life."

Gabriel went to hug his girlfriend. To make her feel more secure, Eleanor imagined.

"I'm sorry if this has all been uncomfortable for you," Gabriel's girlfriend said to Eleanor as she was leaving. "I was just feeling like Gabriel was deceiving me, and I just had to explore this feeling. Gabriel doesn't always tell me things exactly the way they are. He has such a distorted view of life."

Eleanor nodded. "Thank you for sharing that."

"I want you to feel comfortable here," Gabriel's girlfriend said. "I think it's important that Gabriel's friends feel comfortable here. It's his home too. I think it's important he feel comfortable here."

Gabriel's girlfriend smiled at Eleanor. The curl of her lip threw dark shadows on her teeth. Eleanor smiled then hurried home to get rid of her gas.

At her house as Eleanor unpacked the eggs for their party, she hoped the eggs wouldn't give her gas. She thought about inviting Gabriel and his girlfriend to her party, but their idea of a good time seemed different from hers. Perhaps she would gift wrap them some fried eggs and have them delivered to their house. Perhaps they would have a good time dealing with the meaning of her gift.

Petunia waited at the kitchen table while she made a test batch of Morning Thunder. While they got high on the caffeine, she brought tomatoes, zucchini, and spinach in from her garden. She made fried eggs and olive oil dressing. They had sourdough bread and the green corn tamales—all their best and favorite things.

As they looked at the pictures from the newspaper, they told each other stories. Petunia admired people's hats and ties. He thought it was interesting how they had chosen to enclose their faces. Eleanor looked at people's smiles, trying to imagine what lay behind them, what drew the lines in their faces to such hard and peculiar angles. They talked, and they ate, and they had a good time.

After the school year ended, Teddy called. He had never called before. He said the woman he had been living with had just moved out.

"I didn't know you were living with anyone."

"No one did."

"What happened?"

"She beat me up with a rolling pin. I couldn't leave the house for a week."

"So you told her to get out?"

"No. I wanted her to stay."

"Are you okay?"

"Yeah, I got the stitches out, and I'm back at work."

"What did Mom and Dad say?"

"They were mad I wasn't working. They thought I was home drinking or something, so I just let them think that."

"That's good. I mean, it's good you didn't tell them the truth."

"Yeah. I haven't been able to tell anyone. You know, it wasn't until I had to sit here all alone waiting for my face to heal that I realized how wrapped up in my own life I've been. I'm sorry I was never around when you were here."

"Yeah," she responded. It made parts of her life easier to understand.

Then she asked why he called. He wanted her to attend a fortieth-anniversary party for their parents. It was a surprise. Eleanor was surprised, but she agreed to come. It would test her understanding of the human condition.

When she got to her parents' house, she found a note: "Sorry we missed you." They had gone snorkeling in Jamaica. "We thought maybe you were coming home, but we weren't sure. We're never sure what you're going to do." She felt the same way about them. She decided not to take it personally. This was a major revision in her thinking.

She found a college boy living at their house.

"Hey, Julie, come over. There's a great pool here," she heard him say on the phone.

"Hi, I'm Mike," he said when they met in the kitchen.

"I'm Eleanor, the daughter."

"I'm having some friends over for a party. Hope you don't mind."

"Of course not," she lied, looking through the cupboards for something to eat. Eating was still her favorite thing to do when she was home.

She microwaved chocolate pudding and put it over ice cream. She defrosted a container of homemade spaghetti sauce. She preheated the electric range and got steaming water out of the special hot tap and boiled spaghetti. She grated cheese in the automatic shredder. When she went to her mother's, it was like going to Disneyland and staying too long.

She took her food into the dining room and left the mess on the counter for Mike's party. Fortunately, once she got her food on the table, she didn't feel like eating everything. Behavior modification was saving her. She resisted throwing the spaghetti on the walls. She looked up at her high school senior picture and wondered who that strange girl was.

The next day as she walked downtown, she went past the fire station. Fireman Rick was washing a firetruck. As she stopped to say hello, she started to feel crazy.

He was surprised to see her. "I'm divorced now," he said.

"When were you married?" she asked.

"When I was seeing you."

"Oh. Well, it's good you're divorced now."

"Yeah. My girlfriend's pregnant." He looked at his shiny black shoes then smiled at her. "You're looking pretty good these days."

"Yeah. I'm not crazy anymore."

"You shouldn't talk like that."

"Why not? All I need is a pickup and a blow-drier and a husband, and I'll be perfectly normal."

"You shouldn't put yourself down like that. You're okay."

She felt bad that even though she wasn't crazy, people still couldn't understand her.

While her parents were gone, Eleanor decided to call Jamie's old girlfriend, Sharon, who lived in the nearby big city, to talk about Jamie. Sharon still kept in touch with Eleanor's mother.

"No one will talk to me about him," Eleanor said.

Sharon said she could come over.

Sharon was a born-again Christian. A life-size photograph of her husband hung in the family room where they talked. He looked pretty dull and pasty, especially compared to Jamie. Sharon looked pretty dull and pasty too compared to how Eleanor remembered her. Whenever Eleanor opened her mouth, Sharon twitched around the eyes and lips. When Sharon talked, her eyes and lips were fine. Eleanor thought maybe Sharon was afraid she would say something unchristian like "bullshit," a word Jamie had used.

When Eleanor got tired of Sharon twitching, she stopped talking. That warmed Sharon up. She talked about her father, who had been the principal at Eleanor's high school, and people they knew, and people Eleanor didn't know at all. She showed Eleanor the new couch in the living room and took her upstairs to show her the kids' rooms as if Eleanor had come to see her furniture. When Eleanor said she was going to see Jamie's grave, Sharon apologized for never talking about him.

On her way to the cemetery, Eleanor bought some yellow daisies, a flower she thought she remembered Jamie liking. She thought she would be able to locate his plot, but the cemetery looked different from when she was ten, and she couldn't figure it out. She went to the office. Opening the door, she let in the bright sunlight making everybody inside squint. At the counter a secretary was making change for a workman.

The secretary stopped counting the man's change and asked, "Can I help you?"

She tried to say, "I want to see my brother's grave," but she started crying so hard all she could say was, "I, I, I."

The woman looked at her like she was the first person to ever cry in the cemetery office. The man wanted his change counted again. Eleanor nodded, indicating to the woman that she should help the man. When the man and woman were done, Eleanor was able to say she wanted to see her brother's grave and give his name; then, she started crying again.

"When did he die?" the woman asked and started toward the files in the front of the office.

Eleanor stopped crying long enough to say, "Fifteen years ago."

The woman looked at her. Eleanor hadn't thought about how strange it would seem for her to still be crying.

The woman went into the back room. Finally she came out and told the workman where the grave was. Eleanor followed him outside, got the flowers from her car, and walked behind him, keeping at a distance. It was clear the man did not want her close to him.

When she reached the grave, there was a little plaque in the ground with Jamie's name and dates. "Our Beloved Jamie" was inscribed on it. Next to him was their grandmother's grave. Eleanor thought of how her entire family—cousins, aunts, and uncles—had gathered without her. Whatever they had been told about why she was not present, it was a fiction.

She put the flowers on Jamie's grave. She had forgotten to bring a vase and water. She stood crying for a while. She was embarrassed because she was so tall and the graveyard was so flat everyone there could see her crying, so she sat on the grave though no one else was sitting. She gazed at the dusty farmlands spread out below her, the arid mountains behind her, and the brown lawn around her. Everything was less impressive than when she was ten. She tried to talk to Jamie, but as usual he didn't answer. She stood up and wandered into the Mason's section of the cemetery. Their mystical symbols set in a large sundial was the most interesting spot. She had thought something might happen, but nothing did, except now she wasn't afraid to go to her brother's grave. She drove away, sorry the flowers wouldn't last and be enjoyed by anyone.

That evening she visited Jamie's best friend, Sean, who also lived in the big city. He was single and nice-looking, tall and slender like Jamie was. As they sat on the couch he said when he, Jamie, and their friends would go away to high school football games they would go to the other high school's dance afterward and dance with the girls from the opposing team until they got caught and thrown out. He always felt protective of Jamie, like something bad could happen to him.

Sean said he was supposed to have been in the car the day of the accident, but at the last minute he changed his mind. One reason he never visited her family was that her father made him feel guilty, like he should have been the one to die.

When she reached over to kiss him, thinking they could be boyfriend and girlfriend and everything would come full circle, he said he thought of her as a little sister. In the dim light his skin looked strangely pink like Jamie's had in his coffin, and she was glad to get away.

*You were supposed to be psychotic*, Altea had said. *You were the identified crazy one. But you know, every family has problems. Your family would not have seemed unusual if your brother would not have died. That was the only unusual thing. Your parents are not bad people. In fact, they're very lovable. They can't be all bad, they had you. And they had your brothers, and you are all very lovable. Your mother is adorable, and your father is a good man. They've been good members of their community. They've tried hard. They had a lot of pain of their own. We will never know what happened to Jamie. They didn't deliberately murder him. It was an accident.*

When her parents came home, Eleanor listened to how their vacation had been so she didn't have to tell them about hers. While she was listening, she began eating ice cream.

"There's a place for everything, and everything in its place," her mother said because Eleanor hadn't put the empty ice cream carton in the garbage can.

Eleanor wanted to crawl into the garbage can. Maybe her mother would wonder, "If Eleanor's place is in the garbage can, then where does that leave me?" But Eleanor was tired of trying to make her mother think. It never turned out very well.

"Why don't you ever have girls live here?" she asked as her mother folded Mike's laundry.

"Don't we?"

"No. You only help boys."

"Boys seem to need more help, I suppose. Girls have it so

much easier, don't you think?"

"No."

"Now, let's not talk like that."

"Well, around here, all the women are glamorous, and all the men are rich, and I'm neither," she said.

"You could be glamorous if you worked at it, dear. But we love you just the way you are."

Eleanor wondered how that could be possible—not that she was impossible to love, but how could it be possible for them to know the way she was? If they tried to understand her, they might get confused and explode; then, she would have no family at all.

Eleanor had told Teddy she wanted to have some family photos made into posters for the party, so one afternoon when her mother was out, Eleanor dug through the old photographs. Buried at the bottom of the box were pictures of a lively angelic little girl from the age of about one until about four when she got fat and unhappy, the age Eleanor was when her father stopped picking her up because she was "too big" and it made him uncomfortable. She had seen the fat unhappy pictures, but she wasn't sure who the other ones were. They weren't labeled. Her parents had baby pictures of Jamie and Teddy in their room. She thought there weren't any of her because she had been too ugly.

She didn't recognize her own features until she took the pictures into the bathroom and caught odd glimpses of herself in the mirror. She remembered when she was born, Jamie had their mother bring her to school for show-and-tell because he was so proud of her and wanted the world to know. She cried thinking of that little girl who had been lost and of what it must have taken to kill her off. She wanted her back. She wanted to have a little girl like that to love. But the little girl was her, and there would not be another like her.

*Mothers are always envious of the youth and beauty of their daughters*, Altea had said.

That evening Teddy and the girlfriend who beat him up came over. They were engaged now.

Eleanor wanted to show them the photos.

"Don't get out those pictures," her mother said. She hated remembering the past.

Her father called out, "What are you doing?"

"I'm getting out the family pictures," Eleanor said.

He had no comment. He wasn't going to get involved.

She got out the box and took it into the living room. Her parents stayed in the den watching TV.

Eleanor picked the cutest ones of Teddy to show to his fiancée and ones that included Jamie. The fiancée knew about Jamie but had not seen pictures of him. As calm as anything she said how good-looking Jamie had been, and how cute they all were, and laughed at the stories Eleanor told. Altea had said it was normal for brothers to be together and leave their little sisters out. *If your brother wouldn't have died, you would have all grown up and been friends and none of this would be happening.*

In the pictures with all three kids, Eleanor always stood closest to Jamie, touching him. He didn't touch her back, but he allowed her to touch him. In the shots of the whole family, she and Jamie were the only ones looking at each other, the only ones with any connection between them.

Eleanor looked up. Her mother was standing over the box wanting to see the pictures. She started picking them up, smiling, and telling stories.

"'She's my spunky girl.' That's what your brother Jamie used to say about you," her mother said.

"What?" Eleanor asked.

"He always called you his 'spunky girl.'"

"When? When did he say that?" She had only a vague memory of it.

"Oh, when you were two or three."

The age of that little girl she had found in those pictures: *My spunky girl.* So Jamie had known who she was. That was why his death had mattered so much. No one else in her family could see her.

"When you were born, you were so beautiful I said you would be Miss America," her mother recalled.

Then her father came in. He couldn't stand to be left out. He picked up pictures of Jamie and talked about Jamie's band playing in the garage.

"Those were the best days of my life," he said.

*It was their pain that kept your parents silent,* Altea had said. *It was their only way of handling their grief.* They did not forget him as Eleanor thought they had.


At the anniversary party there were over two hundred guests—family and friends converging at a park. White tables and red balloons were scattered around. In the center was a gazebo with the white cake and the posters of the family pictures.

To go with the pictures, Eleanor had written her parents' life story. Each child got one paragraph. She was afraid someone would cut the paragraph she wrote about Jamie, but no one did. In the end, this was his story:

"Jamie played clarinet and saxophone. He was the drum major in junior high and his senior year in high school. He also had his own band, Lost Celestials, which played frequently for high school dances. He played in the college jazz band while still a high school student. He dreamed of being a high school music teacher. He was killed in a car accident when he was eighteen."

It was just one paragraph in five pages. It helped Eleanor to see him in the context of the years of her parents' lives, the years of their marriage, the years of their family since his death.

As Teddy began the ceremonies, her mother gave her a dirty look. Earlier Teddy had cut Eleanor out of the program, afraid she would be too emotional.

"It'll be okay," Eleanor reassured her mother who had not acknowledged her all day.

Teddy made a toast to their mother, "who has given us nothing but pleasure, while we have given her nothing but hell." Their mother rolled her eyes. For their father, Teddy toasted the man "who smiles when things go smoothly and when everything goes dead wrong." Their father nodded.

Eleanor reminded herself, *I am the one who is dangerous. I am the one who tells.*

Next came the roast, delivered by their father's closest friend.

"I like to roast," he began. "I am good at roasting. I am often called on at events like this to roast. And I was pleased when Teddy asked me to do this roast today. But all week long I've been thinking, 'What can I possibly say that is bad about James and Helene?' and I couldn't think of one thing. The rest of us gossip.

James and Helene don't gossip. The rest of us tell lies. James and Helene don't lie. The rest of us are mean to our children. James and Helene are never mean to their children."

*I am the one who is dangerous. I am the one who tells,* Eleanor repeated in her head.

"All I can say is I am glad to be here and to have James and Helene as part of our community."

Everyone applauded. Eleanor's father looked satisfied. Her mother looked shocked. She had pulled it off better than she thought.

Eleanor repeated, *They don't gossip, they don't lie, and they are not mean to their children.* The illusion was holding. As long as she didn't say anything, it would not crack. No wonder her parents were stone to her.

*Feel sympathy for them,* Altea had insisted. *They don't feel they can let anyone know who they really are. You do not want them to fall apart. You do not want to expose them. You do not want to have to deal with that.*


The day Eleanor was leaving, Teddy pulled up at the convenience store as she was getting gas.

"Hi," she said. She waved at him and went in to pay.

"Hi," he said when she came out. "When are you leaving?"

"Now."

"I'm sorry I didn't get to see more of you. I didn't think you were leaving so soon." He hugged her.

She started to say "I love you," but thinking of it made her start to cry so she didn't.

"Bye," he said when they stopped hugging.

"Bye," she said.

She stopped by the construction company office to say goodbye to her father.

He hugged her and said, "I think you're doing just fine, honey. I know you'll be okay."

She smiled. It was the first time he seemed to know anything good about her.

She went home to tell her mother goodbye. Eleanor said she had seen Teddy, and he had given her a hug.

"Really? He won't hug me anymore. He doesn't seem to want to have anything to do with me, so I just leave him alone. I have to respect what he wants. He's a grown man now, you know."

Eleanor nodded. She realized why her mother liked clichés. They were like presents of thought.

While she finished packing her car, her mother brought out bags of oranges and cookies for her.

"I'm so sorry we didn't get to see more of you," her mother said. "We miss you, you know."

Eleanor nodded.

"I love you," her mother said.

"I know." Now Eleanor was almost crying.

She hugged her beautiful mother tightly, and, sorry nothing could ever be like either of them wanted, she got into her car and drove off into her life.

**M. Kaat Toy (Katherine Toy Miller)** *of Taos, New Mexico, has a Ph.D. in English (creative writing--fiction) from Florida State University where she studied with Virgil Suarez, Mark Winegardner, and Robert Olen Butler and an M.F.A. in creative writing (fiction) from the University of Arizona where she studied with Edward Abbey and worked on this novel with Vance Bourjaily, C. E. Poverman, and Francine Prose.*